SPEED DATING

PRESTON'S MILL

NOELLE ADAMS

SAMANTHA CHASE

Isabella Warren was trying not to get annoyed with Mrs. Pendergast as she briskly brushed on color and folded foils in the elderly woman's hair.

Her attempt was gradually failing.

Mrs. Pendergast had been one of her very first clients when Isabella had started at the salon six year ago, and the old woman still came in every week for an appointment to get "coiffed and buffed"—as she called getting her hair and nails done. Isabella appreciated the loyalty and was fond of all her clients.

But every few weeks Mrs. Pendergast would use the opportunity to give Isabella an hour-long lecture on how she needed to get her life together.

Isabella thought her life was mostly together. She was twenty-five years old and a part owner of the beauty salon, so she made decent money—certainly more than enough to support herself in a small town. She rented a nice one-bedroom apartment above the coffee shop downtown, just a block away from the salon. And she had a lot of friends and got along well with her family.

Her life might not be extraordinary in any way, but she had done just fine for herself so far.

She didn't, however, have a husband—or even a boyfriend—and to Mrs. Pendergast, that signified the need for a lecture.

Today the lecture was on how she couldn't keep waiting around to find a man and how, when Isabella's sister Tori got married in a few months, Isabella would be the only one of the four Warren sisters left unmarried.

"But Mrs. Pendergast," Isabella broke in, finally unable to just listen in silence. "I do date whenever I can. There aren't that many available men in town, you know."

She'd lived in Preston, Virginia, for most of her life, so she was used to the small-town atmosphere and everyone knowing her business. She'd gone out with three different men in the past year—never for more than a few dates—and each time she'd faced endless inquisitions afterward about what had happened and what had gone wrong.

She added, "I haven't found the right man yet."

"That's just an excuse, dear. I hear it all the time from young women like you. You think the right man will magically appear and that there's nothing you can do to hurry him along in the meantime. But men aren't the way they used to be. They used to have backbones, you know. They used to *pursue* a woman. Now they've gotten spoiled and wait for girls to make moves on them."

"Spoiled," Mrs. Henson repeated from where she sat in the chair next to Isabella's station. "They're used to getting what they want without trying. It's a whole different world from when I was a girl. I read magazines and watch TV, you know. If you want a man, you've got to put yourself out there."

Elise, Isabella's partner in the salon, was working on Mrs. Henson's hair, and she met Isabella's eyes in the mirror with a look of suppressed amusement.

Isabella cleared her throat. "How do you suggest I put myself out there?"

"Firstly, you need to not spend so much time with that young man," Mrs. Pendergast said.

Isabella blinked. "You mean Jace?"

"Yes, that's the one."

"But he's my best friend."

"Perhaps, but what man is going to ask you out when you're always with another man?"

"But there's nothing romantic between me and Jace. Everyone knows that. *Everyone* knows that."

Elise laughed. "Everyone knows, but not everyone believes."

"But there's really not! We've always only been friends. And I'm not going to drop my best friend just because a potential date might feel threatened."

Mrs. Pendergast didn't argue, but she shook her head and tsked her tongue, which was almost as annoying as a verbal response would have been.

Isabella bit her lip and made herself resist the urge to

3

keep arguing. She'd had to explain the nature of her friendship with Jace so many times since high school that it wasn't really worth the effort anymore.

"Be that as it may, you still need to put yourself out there. Everything I hear is about The Internet," Mrs. Pendergast said, pronouncing the last words in a way that made it clear they were capitalized—as if she were referring to a deep, dark, unknown force.

"Online dating," Mrs. Henson agreed, nodding vigorously in a way that required Elise to step back with her scissors. "I hear about it on the shows. That's the way it's done nowadays."

"I've got a cousin who met her husband online," Elise added with a half smile, slanting a mischievous look at Isabella that made it clear she knew exactly what she was doing in mentioning it.

Isabella groaned. "Not you too."

"Nothing's wrong with online dating," Elise said. She was a couple of years older than Isabella and already had three children. "I'm surprised you haven't tried it before."

Isabella shrugged. "I've thought about it. It just seemed... I don't know. Not really like *me*."

"How do you know what's like you until you've tried it?" Mrs. Pendergast demanded. "Now that we're agreed, who knows how The Internet works?"

The sound of laughter from the waiting area caused Isabella to turn her head and see that her next client, Michelle Woodward, a former classmate, had been listening in on the conversation. She was pulling a tablet

4

out of her bag. "I can go online. Elise, what dating site did your cousin use to find her husband?"

Isabella finished foiling Mrs. Pendergast's hair in a daze as the women together created a profile for her on the dating site, debating over the best way to describe her and the kind of men she was interested in to complete each of the fields of the profile.

Despite Mrs. Pendergast's high-handedness, Isabella realized the women were mostly teasing her, so she couldn't be too annoyed by the interference and the fun they were having. Eventually she gave up trying to resist and posed for a couple of pictures with exaggerated coyness, which made everyone laugh.

When the profile was complete, they all peered at Michelle's tablet to admire the page. Despite the teasing, Isabella decided it wasn't really a bad profile. She wasn't any sort of beauty queen. She was average-sized with long dark hair, and her best features were her eyes, which were so dark a blue they were almost violet. She'd always taken decent pictures, and the profile expressed a lot of personality.

Maybe joining the dating site wasn't a bad idea. She knew most of the available men in Preston, but there were plenty of towns nearby in eastern Virginia with men she'd never met before.

"Should we publish it?" Michelle asked, checking Isabella's expression.

For a moment, Isabella froze as all the women in the salon stared at her expectantly. Then she finally nodded.

"Sure, why not? I don't have to go out with anyone on the site if no one seems good."

Michelle tapped on the screen to publish the profile, and in the midst of the laughter and excitement, the bell on the salon sounded.

Glancing over, Isabella saw her mother coming in. "Hi, Mom," she said with a smile, hoping the others weren't going to tell her mom about the dating site.

She didn't mind telling her family herself, but she didn't want to make it a big deal.

Her mother came over to kiss Isabella on the cheek, and her dark eyes were blazing with excitement.

"What is it?" Isabella asked. "Good news?"

"Carla had her ultrasound today. I wanted to bring this in to show you."

Carla was Isabella's second-oldest sister, and she was pregnant with her first child. So the conversation about Isabella's dating prospects immediately changed to oohing and aahing over the ultrasound images.

Isabella was happy for her sister. All her sisters. Even her younger sister Tori, who was getting married in three months. But she occasionally felt a little twinge like she'd been left behind.

She wanted to get married and start a family too. She'd dreamed of being a mother since she was four years old. And it was sometimes hard to watch her three sisters all get her dream before she did.

She felt selfish and petty whenever she acknowledged

those feelings though, so she tried very hard not to indulge them.

When her mother finally left the salon, Isabella had made a decision.

Maybe Mrs. Pendergast was right. Maybe she did need to be more intentional in getting what she wanted.

She was going to do the dating site for real. She was going to date as many men as she could until she finally found the right one.

In one way, Mrs. Pendergast had been right.

She didn't have to wait around, doing nothing, hoping for Mr. Right to finally fall in her lap.

If it took a dating marathon to finally find the man she wanted, then that was what she was going to do.

Isabella was sweeping up the salon after her last client of the day when she caught a glimpse of a very handsome man reflected in one of the mirrors.

Her heart leaped in excitement, and she straightened up instinctively, but when she turned around she discovered it was just Jace.

Jace Foster—her cute, familiar, absent-minded best friend since high school.

He had the same rumpled brown hair, hazel eyes, and lean body he'd always had, and he was wearing his glasses this evening, which meant he'd been working so hard he'd forgotten to take them off. He'd worked for the town of

Preston ever since he'd graduated from college. He was absolutely adorable, but she wasn't sure where she'd gotten the idea he was a handsome stranger.

Always glad to see him, she smiled and walked over to give him a hug, still holding the broom in one hand. "Hi! I'm almost finished up here."

"Hi," he murmured, breathing deeply as he wrapped his arms around her, almost like he was smelling her hair.

She pulled away to check his expression, relaxing when he gave her his normal smile.

"You look all excited about something," he said, scanning her face as he dropped his arms.

"I am! I got this brainstorm earlier, and I can't believe I didn't think of it before." She leaned over to sweep the pile of hair, lint, and trash into the dustpan, wanting to finish up quickly so she and Jace could get out of there. "All this time I've been waiting around for the love of my life to fall at my feet."

She'd glanced back at Jace over her shoulder, so she noticed his expression change slightly. "Oh yeah?"

"Yeah. And the answer was right there, staring me in the face the whole time."

Jace's expression changed even more, his whole body tensing slightly. He'd always been a little uncomfortable when she talked about her love life, and she tried to respect his boundaries and comfort zone. But he was her best friend. She had to tell him the things that were important to her. "What's the answer?" he asked, his voice growing a bit hoarse.

8

She was about to reply, turning her head back toward the dustpan. As she did, a big black spider began to crawl over the pile of trash and up onto her hand.

She screamed, shook her hand violently, and ran backward several steps in instinctive panic.

Colliding with Jace, she ended up in his arms.

"What the hell?" he asked urgently, tightening his arms around her and pulling her away from the source of her terror.

"A... a *spider*!"

He relaxed as he realized why she'd panicked, and she could feel rather than see the smile growing on his face.

"Don't you dare laugh!" She checked her hand, rubbing it vigorously even though she must have flung the spider away. "It was *on* me. It was crawling on me!"

She wasn't a particularly squeamish woman about a lot of things, but spiders were her nemesis with their wicked little eyes and all those creepy legs.

Despite her admonishment, Jace chuckled. "Well, it's not on you anymore."

"But it's still here somewhere. Go do your job and find it." She was still huddled up against Jace, and she couldn't help but like the feel of his body against hers.

He'd been skinny and rather geeky in high school, when they'd first become friends. He still tended toward the lean side, but she wasn't sure when he'd gotten so strong and hard and... masculine.

Still laughing, Jace released her and went over to investigate the middle of the floor. Eventually he found the spider and stepped on it. "There. All safe now."

"Thank you," she said, still feeling prickles run up and down her arm. "He doesn't have any comrades still lurking over there, does he?"

Jace shook his head, smiling at her fondly. "No spiders in sight."

She released a breath and slowly walked over to where she'd left her pile of trash. Very hesitantly, she leaned over to finish sweeping it into the dustpan.

"So what were you saying?" Jace asked in a different tone.

"About what?"

"About the love of your life being there all the time, staring you in the face."

Isabella stood up and met Jace's eyes. He was staring at her strangely, seeming tense for no good reason. Her breath caught in her throat, and she couldn't look away.

"Isabella?" he prompted, a rough texture in his voice.

"What?"

"What's been staring you in the face?"

Realizing she was acting like an idiot, she shook her head to dispel the daze. It must be the aftermath of her panic over the spider causing her to respond that way to Jace's look. "Oh. It's not the love of my life. It's just the answer."

His brow wrinkled. "What's the answer?"

"The salon ladies were teasing me earlier about me being the only one in my family not getting married and having babies yet," she explained. "And how there's only three months left until Tori's wedding, and then I'll be the only Warren girl left."

"You can't let them make you feel bad about that."

"I know. But I do want to get married, and I've just been waiting around, expecting the man to magically appear. They jokingly made me a profile on a dating site. I was annoyed at first, but then I realized, why not?"

"Why not what?"

"Join the dating site. Start actively looking for the love of my life, instead of just waiting around."

"So you're going to do a dating site? That's your big revelation?" There was an edge to his voice now that was half-skeptical and half something else. If she didn't know better, she would say it was disappointment.

"Don't make it sound silly. I want to find a man, so I'm going to find one."

"On a dating site?"

"Why not? I haven't had much luck here in Preston. I need to branch out and try new things."

He shook his head and took the dustpan out of her hand, dumping the contents into the trash. "Okay. Good luck with that."

He didn't sound excited. At all.

Isabella frowned. "You could be a little supportive, you know."

"I'll be supportive," he said, almost resignedly. He pushed his glasses farther up his nose. "So what's the plan?"

Isabella perked up. "I have three months until Tori's wedding. I'm going to go out with as many men as possible in that time. If all goes well, in three months, I'll have found the right man to bring to her wedding."

Jace's mouth dropped open slightly. "You think you're going to find someone in three months?"

"Maybe. Maybe not. The point is to give myself a deadline so I really take it seriously. It will be like a dating marathon."

"A dating..."

"Marathon. If I'm going to do this, then I've got to do it right. I haven't had a serious relationship since Brock, and at the rate things are going, I might never end up with anyone. No more sitting around for me." She smiled at him, feeling a well of excitement at the idea of doing something intentional and productive to pursue a relationship. "What do you think?"

Jace was still staring at her strangely. "I think... okay."

She shook her head at him. "That's the best you can do? You're supposed to be my best friend, you know."

"I know. I am." He took a visible breath. "I am."

"Good." She walked over to rub his arm. "You should really consider doing the same thing. Maybe you can find the love of your life in three months too."

"Right. The love of my life. Right."

He was definitely in a strange mood today, Isabella thought as she finished sweeping the floor.

~

A couple of hours later, Isabella was carrying plates back to the kitchen from where she and Jace had eaten on the floor of the living room.

Jace was still acting a little strange—not as relaxed as he normally was when they hung out. She hoped everything was okay with him.

Now that she'd had enough to time to think it through, she was really excited about her dating plan. After all, it was better to *do* something about getting what she wanted than sit around and mope because nothing ever happened to her. But her concern about Jace's strange behavior was getting in the way of some of her excitement.

She gave the plates a quick rinse and put them in the dishwasher—since Jace had made dinner, she thought it was only fair to clean up for him—and then she returned to the living room.

Jace was on the floor, slouching back against the couch. His long legs were stretched out, and something about the set of his shoulders looked tired, almost glum.

She frowned, her chest tightening in both concern and affection. She hated to see him look like that.

She was trying to think of something encouraging to say when her phone chirped. Picking it up from the coffee table automatically, she blinked when she saw she had six messages from the dating site.

Six different men were interested in connecting.

"What is it?" Jace asked, evidently reading her expression.

"Wow. Things move really fast with this site." She

smiled and lowered herself to sit beside him, showing him the messages on her phone. "Look at all these guys."

"Well, what did you expect?" Jace asked after a minute, sounding slightly gruff. "You're gorgeous. Of course, they're going to be interested. But don't jump into anything too quickly. You know there are going to be creeps on sites like this, don't you?"

"Of course I do." She couldn't help but flush with pleasure at his calling her gorgeous, despite his less than encouraging comments. "I'm not going to jump into anything without being careful. And I'll have you for big brotherly advice on vetting every potential date. I'm not too worried."

She'd reached over to ruffle his hair, feeling very fond despite his grumpy mood. But his body clenched strangely, and she felt a little awkward at her affectionate gesture, so she pulled her hand away.

Clearly she'd need to wait to talk about her dating prospects until Jace was in a better mood.

2

GREAT. JUST GREAT.

Isabella was going to start dating. Actively dating. Like... men coming and taking her out all the time dating.

Fan-freaking-tastic.

Not.

For the most part, Jace had held it together until Isabella had left. That meant he'd had to hold his tongue for a lot longer than he wanted while she made awkward small talk about the guys who were already reaching out to her for dates.

He hated them all already.

Why now? Why did she now—all of a sudden—have to get into this dating zone. Hell, if she had just given him a bit longer, he would have finally asked her out. Really! Pacing the room, Jace kept telling himself that he would have done it. Soon. Really soon.

Well... eventually.

He'd been thinking about it for a while, and he had been confident that he was ready to do it. Or... almost ready to do it. Or...

"Dammit!" he muttered.

So maybe he'd been procrastinating and overthinking this for a while. Okay, years. But how was he supposed to just throw it out there that he was hopelessly and completely in love with Isabella when it meant that she could completely reject him? Then he'd not only lose any hope of having a romantic relationship with her, but he'd also lose his best friend. It wasn't a risk he was willing to take—at least not take lightly.

And now look where he was.

Having to sit back and watch while she went on a dating marathon to find her perfect man.

Me! I'm the perfect man for her! Just why... why can't she see it?

The problem was him. Jace knew that. He was quiet and shy and never wanted to do anything to rock the boat. They were comfortable with one another, and even though they'd known each other since high school and he felt that he knew everything there was to know about Isabella, he was still afraid of doing anything to jeopardize what they had together.

Then there was Brock, who had dated Isabella all through high school. Jace and Brock had been fairly tight in school—that's how he and Isabella had become such good friends—and on some level, it just seemed awkward to make a play on a friend's ex.

Even if that ex was a complete and total jackass.

Yeah, that had really turned into more of an issue than Jace had ever imagined. At first, he had felt ashamed of his feelings for Isabella since she was dating a guy who was supposed to be his friend. Then he'd settled in and accepted the fact that he'd never be with Isabella in the way he wanted.

But then Brock had cheated and Isabella had been free.

True, it had taken years for that to happen—or at least for Isabella to find out about all the times Brock had cheated—but at least she'd found out at last.

Unfortunately, by that time Jace had been utterly and completely locked into the friend zone. Not that it was a bad place to be. He just didn't want to be there forever and had hoped that Isabella would eventually come to discover that he was the one for her.

But she hadn't.

And apparently never would.

"Shit," he muttered, raking a hand through his hair. "Now what?"

There was no time to give it more of a thought because there was a knock on his door. With a heavy sigh, he walked over and pulled it open. And froze.

"Oh, uh, hey." Standing in the doorway was his sister Erin, holding a very large… "Um, what is that?" he asked, nodding toward the covered case in her hands.

"Nice to see you too, Jace," Erin said with a grin as she stepped around him and into the apartment. "I really appreciate you doing this for me. Dale and I are so excited about this trip, and Beau was the only thing tripping us up. So you are truly a lifesaver. Thank you."

Slowly Jace closed the door and took in his sister's words and racked his brain for what the hell she was talking about.

It didn't take Erin long to figure out that he was still confused. With a bit of fanfare, she pulled the sheet off the case she was carrying, and Jace saw it was actually a cage. With a bird in it.

Shit. He'd totally forgotten.

"Erin, I, uh..."

"This is Beau!" she said cheerily and then squatted down so she could be eye level with the bird. "And he's a handsome boy! Isn't he? Who's a handsome boy?"

Jace just stared at the bird in the cage, colored in bright blues and greens.

Erin stood and studied her brother for a moment before crossing her arms over her chest and making a tsking sound at him. "You totally forgot about this, didn't you?"

What was the point in lying? "Yes."

Rolling her eyes, she put her large purse down on the sofa and began pulling out papers and bags of food. "I don't have a whole lot of time because I need to get home and finish packing. Our flight tomorrow leaves really early in the morning so pay attention."

"Erin, maybe this isn't the best idea. I'm totally not prepared for this, and... honestly, it's not the best time right now."

God, he hated how pathetic he sounded!

Erin froze for a minute, and her gaze narrowed. "Why? What's going on with you?" With a sigh, she sat down next to her purse.

"Didn't you just say you don't have a lot of time?"

"Jace, could you for once just say what's on your mind and not make me work for it?"

"Fine." He told her all about Isabella's dating marathon plan. His sister had known for years about his feelings for his best friend, so none of this came as a shock to her. "How am I supposed to sit back and let this happen?"

"You don't," she said simply.

"What?"

"You get out there and throw your hat into the ring and get off your ass and do something! Seriously, Jace. It's time."

"But how? And what if she's not interested? What if I finally do this, and she freaks out and then ends up hating me?"

Reaching over to take one of his hands in hers, Erin squeezed it. "Sweetie, that is a risk we all take. But it's time you at least tried. This has been going on for years, and it's time for you to find out where you stand. If it's going to happen, great. If it's not, then you can finally move on, because—believe it or not—we'd all like to see you settled too."

"Oh God," he groaned.

She nodded and then smiled. "Uh, yeah. We've all been patient, and I've had to talk Mom off the ledge a time or two where you're concerned, but you're not getting any younger either, and I'd love it if you could take some of the pressure off me and Dale and find someone that Mom can harp on about grandchildren."

This was so not the conversation he wanted to be having.

Ever.

"So the bird…"

Erin took the hint. "Beau. And he is just going to make you fall in love with him! He's an Amazon parrot. He's a good boy, and let me tell you he's extremely playful! You just need to pay attention to his body language to figure out how he's feeling. For example, his feathers will all go up and out if he's excited about something."

"Excited? What the hell could he be excited about? He's a bird. Sitting in a cage."

Erin leveled him with a glare. "Don't talk like that about him!"

"Seriously?"

Ignoring him, she went on with her lecture on Beau. "I've brought his food with him, but he'll expect to get some people food as well."

Jace looked at her with disbelief.

"It's true. He loves to hang out at the table and have whatever Dale and I are eating. It's adorable. He's really part of the family, and you should let him have dinner with you too."

Jace decided to keep it to himself that that particular scenario was never going to happen.

"And then there's his bath," Erin continued with a smile toward the bird. "He really loves a bath, and you can really do it however you want. He can get in the shower with you, or you can give him a spray bath. Or you can just give him a bowl of water and he'll splash around in it."

"There is no way that bird is taking a shower with me!" Jace had reached the end of his rope with this ridiculousness. "I'll feed him—in his cage—and let him... splash around in his water dish, but I draw the line at taking a bath with him!"

"Don't be so dramatic. It's not like you have to share a bubble bath by candlelight. Sheesh. All I'm saying is that it's not such a bad thing to just let him... hang out in the shower with you."

Jace shook his head. "No."

With a huff, Erin handed him the sheets of paper she had pulled out of her bag earlier. "Fine. Whatever. Here is a complete list of his likes and dislikes and general care and directions." She jumped to her feet and picked up her purse. "Don't be an ass to my bird."

As much as Jace wanted to give her some sort of snarky retort, he just didn't have it in him. The bird was the least of his problems. In a few days, Beau would be gone, and he'd still be struggling to come up with a way to convince

Isabella that her plan to become some sort of serial dater wasn't smart.

"Okay. I think that's everything!" Erin made her way toward the door. "We really appreciate this. You have no idea how badly Dale and I need this trip."

"So you'll be back... Saturday? Sunday?" For the life of him, Jace really couldn't remember anything about his sister's travel plans.

Erin looked at him oddly.

And then a slow smile crossed her face.

"Sunday," she said, smiling.

"Oh. Okay. Sunday. Four days. Great."

Then she stepped in closer. "Not this Sunday, Jace."

"Sooo... next Sunday."

She shook her head.

And then it hit him. "Seriously? You're going to be away for two weeks?"

"Ding, ding, ding! You got it!"

"And when did I agree to this?" he demanded, all traces of humor gone. "I might have forgotten having a conversation, but I know I did not agree to bird sitting for two weeks. Uh-uh. No way."

"Remember the barbecue Dale and I hosted last month?"

"Yeah. Pool party. Burgers, ribs. There's no way I would have agreed to this. The ribs weren't that good."

Erin shrugged. "No, but you were, shall we say, a little distracted by a certain someone in a bathing suit."

Jace's eyes went wide. "You are just... just..."

"Just?"

"The devil. You're the devil."

That made her laugh. "Maybe. But I get the job done." She looked at her watch and then back at him. "But now I really have to go. Take care of Beau, and I'll call to check on him."

"Erin! Wait!"

"It's too late—you're stuck bird sitting. I have no other options!"

"It's not that," he said with a weary sigh. "I just... What do I do? How do I convince Isabella to not..."

"Date?"

He nodded.

"You're going to have to put some serious effort into wooing her."

"Wooing? Really? That's a thing?"

She nodded. "A pretty important one."

"I don't even know what it means!"

Sighing loudly, Erin's shoulders sagged with defeat. "Jace, romantic gestures. Talking to her about how you feel. Be honest with her, and quit dragging your feet on this. Because if you don't step up and let her know how much she means to you, some other guy is going to swoop in and sweep her off her feet."

"Yeah, but..."

"Sweetie, I really have to go!" Leaning in, she kissed him on the cheek. "You're going to be fine."

"Somehow I doubt that. If she turns me down... if she's

not interested... I'm gonna be alone. There's no one else that I want to be with."

Reaching up, she cupped his cheek. "You're not going to be alone, Jace."

Hope sprang up in his chest. "You really think so?"

"You'll have Beau."

Yeah. His sister was the devil.

Spending the night with the bird wasn't the worst thing in the world.

It was actually a really good distraction.

He talked, the bird listened, and really it was kind of helpful.

But now by the light of a new day, Jace had to face the fact that the person he had to start talking to was *not* a bird. For starters, the bird agreed with everything that he said without talking back or disagreeing.

He had a feeling it was going to be a completely different scenario once he started showing Isabella how he felt.

It was Thursday, and they normally went out for pizza on Thursdays after work. His plan was to up his game and take her someplace nice. Special. Romantic. Then, over dinner, he'd talk about how much she meant to him and how much he appreciated her and then transition to where he saw them heading together in the future.

Easy.

Simplicity at its finest.

Beau had seemed to think it was a good place to start, if all his nodding was a sign.

As he got ready for work, Jace ran every scenario in his mind about how Isabella would respond. There was the obvious and most-wished-for choice of her being thrilled and admitting that she felt the same about him.

That had him smiling.

Then there was the possibility of her being disgusted by his suggestion of them being more than friends. He envisioned her tossing a plate of spaghetti at him and then doing the same with a glass of red wine—because the combination would leave a lasting stain to remind him of his total humiliation—and her storming out of the restaurant and demanding that he never speak to her again.

Less smiling and feeling a little like throwing up at that one.

And then there was the middle ground which—honestly—was no better than being rejected. It was her smiling at him patiently and telling him how he'd always been like a brother to her. And then, because he was a glutton for punishment, he pictured their waiter being some sort of male-underwear-model type who would charm her and share that he was also a veterinarian whose specialty was special-needs animals and Isabella would leave with him. Of course she'd ask Jace if he minded, and he'd say no.

Because he was a schmuck like that.

They'd leave together—her and Mr. Saving-the-World-

One-Injured-Animal-at-a-Time—and he'd hear her talking about what a great buddy Jace was.

That wasn't anything new. She said it all the time, but somehow Jace knew in this scenario it would just... well, it would hurt.

A lot.

Looking at his reflection, he shook his head and did his best to clear it. "Positive. Think positive. It's all going to be okay. We're stronger than this, and no matter what, we'll make it work."

That was his mantra all through the day. Whenever he felt his resolve slipping or negative thoughts creeping in, Jace simply reminded himself that everything was going to be okay. By the time he showed up at the salon, he was feeling pretty damn good. He'd picked up a bouquet of Isabella's favorite flowers—tulips—and had gotten them a reservation at her favorite Italian restaurant.

He couldn't wait to see the surprised look on her face.

When he walked inside, she smiled at him, and everything in him softened and relaxed.

"Hey, beautiful," he said as he approached. She had worked all day. Her makeup was a little faded, and her hair was a little disheveled, and yet she was the most beautiful woman he had ever seen.

"Hey, you!" she said happily. "What do you have there?"

Jace held out the bouquet to her. "Just a little something special for you."

Gasping, she readily took the flowers and held them to

her face to smell them. "Oh, Jace! What a great surprise! Thank you! You know how much I love... ouch!"

"Are you all right?" he asked, instantly concerned.

"No!" she cried. "I think... oh my God! I think I just got stung!"

He swatted the bouquet from her hands, and sure enough, he saw something fly away and saw a small red bump on her cheek. Reaching out to touch it, Isabella pushed his hand away. "I just want to look at it," he said softly, doing his best to not alarm her but to no avail.

Turning away, Isabella ran over to a mirror to look at the mark and then cursed. Looking over at Elise—who was finishing up for the day too—she asked, "What do I do?"

"I think I have some Benadryl, and you should put some ice on that," Elise replied. "Give me a minute. Why don't you sit and relax?" And then she ran to the back room.

Jace walked over, feeling horrible. This was not the way he had hoped to start off their night. "Bella, I'm so sorry! I... I don't even know what to say!"

She gave him a weak smile and waved him off. "Oh, stop. It's not your fault. It was just a... freakish accident. I'll be fine."

But he knew she wouldn't. She'd say she was, but he knew how much she hated bugs. Plus it had to hurt, and now the medicine would make her sleepy. With a sigh, he resigned himself to the fact that tonight was not going to be his night.

When Elise came out of the back room, she handed

Isabella a tablet, some water, and then an ice pack. Jace held her hand, and within minutes he already noticed her eyes going a little soft and heavy.

Another sigh.

Standing, he took her by the hand. "Come on. Let's get you home."

"But it's pizza night," she protested around a very loud yawn.

Jace chuckled. "I'll call our order in."

"But..."

He shook his head, passed Elise the ice pack, and then handed Isabella her purse. "I'm walking you home right now."

She yawned again. "Those pills lie. Nondrowsy, my ass."

He tucked her in at his side and placed a gentle kiss on her forehead. "Yup. Has nothing to do with you being a lightweight."

She laughed softly and hugged him and then grabbed her bouquet on their way out the door. "Thank you for my flowers. And tulips. My favorite." She sighed happily. "You're the best. You know me so well."

"That I do."

"I just hope when I meet my perfect man that he remembers all the little things like you do." She looked up at him with a sleepy smile. "And if he doesn't, you'll remind him, right?"

For a moment, he could only stare at her. But she

looked so hopeful and happy that, hell, what could he possibly say?"

"Of course I will," he said, his voice gruff.

Isabella hugged him close again. "And that's why you're the best."

Shit. This definitely wasn't his night.

3

THE FOLLOWING FRIDAY, AFTER ELEVEN IN THE EVENING, Isabella knocked on the door to Jace's apartment, hoping he hadn't yet gone to bed.

She should have called first to make sure, but she'd been so frustrated after her date—the first one she'd arranged from the dating site—that she'd headed right over to his place.

That was always her first instinct. To go see Jace.

His building was called Preston's Mill. It was a converted mill—the historic building redone to house beautifully designed apartments. Isabella had loved it ever since he'd moved in a couple of years ago. She sometimes thought about moving into the building herself, but it was a lot more expensive then the little place she rented and not nearly as conveniently located to the salon.

Jace opened the door after a minute, his expression turned down in a frown that she knew was one of surprise.

"Is everything all right?" he asked, his voice a bit hoarse. He wore sweat pants and a gray T-shirt with a yellow duck on the front. She'd bought the shirt for him a couple of years ago because she'd thought it was cute.

"Yeah. Sorry to just come over. Is it too late?"

"You don't have to be sorry. Of course it's not too late." He stepped to the side to let her in. "Are you okay? Did something happen on your date?"

She sighed. "No. Nothing. I mean, *nothing*."

His face relaxed as they walked farther into the apartment. Isabella slumped onto a stool at the kitchen bar and dropped her purse on the floor at her feet.

Jace went to the refrigerator to get two bottles of water. "He wasn't into you?"

"I guess he was. Maybe. But he was so incredibly boring that I couldn't tell if he was interested in anything at all."

Chuckling, Jace handed her the water and leaned against the countertop across from her. "Sounds like a winner."

"He seemed like a decent guy over email, but in person he was *so boring*." A rustle beside her caught her attention, and she noticed that the parrot Jace was pet sitting was perched on the back of a dining room chair, looking at her inquisitively. Smiling, she grabbed a grape from a bowl on the counter and extended her hand to offer it to him. The bird snatched it up enthusiastically.

"What did he talk about?" Jace asked.

"That was part of the problem. He didn't seem to be

able to make any conversation on his own, so I had to lead the discussion all the time. But whenever I asked him a direct question, he'd go off on a long, tedious answer about everything he knew on the topic." She made a face. "*So boring.*"

Beau had flapped over to perch on the stool beside her, so she gave him another grape. Jace hadn't been all that excited about taking care of the parrot, but she thought he was lovely with the vivid greens and blues of his feathers. She liked his bright eyes and the way he cocked his head as if he were listening to them.

"You should have heard him," she continued after a pause. "First, I had to hear about who he thought would win the Grammy awards this year—with all these quotes from reviews and columns he'd read. Then I had to hear about the history of toilets."

"Toilets?"

"Yes, toilets!" Despite her exasperation, she giggled softly. "And let me tell you, there are some details about the early days of toilets that I really didn't need to know."

"I would imagine so."

"And then there was twenty-two minutes on different kinds of wine and how they're made. Twenty-two minutes! I actually timed it. It was *so* boring!"

"Well, I guess that's what happens when you hook up with someone online."

She frowned at the evident skepticism and amusement in his tone. "Don't be a downer. It was just my first date. I'm sure the other dates will be better."

Jace's brows drew together. "What other dates?"

"I've got a date tomorrow and then one next Friday. Things are happening fast. I should have tried online dating a long time ago. I just hope these other guys aren't *so boring*."

"So... ring," Beau squawked from beside her.

She and Jace both gasped and jerked to look at the bird. When she realized what he'd said, she repeated, "So boring," very slowly and handed the bird a grape.

"So bo-ring," Beau squawked, reaching out for another grape before she'd managed to retrieve her hand.

She laughed in delight and handed him three more grapes as he repeated the words each time.

"Why didn't you tell me he could talk?" she demanded, when Jace finally took the grapes away, muttering about not encouraging poultry to rise above their station.

"Erin said he could, but he hasn't said a word the whole time he's been here. He's just made loud squawks. I thought she was making it up."

"He's brilliant! We should teach him to say something really funny."

"I really don't want him chattering all the time."

Her chest tightened at the adorably grumpy expression on his face, and she reached out to push his hair back from his forehead. "Don't be grouchy about the poor bird. It's not his fault your sister stuck you with him."

"I know." He seemed to lean into her hand for a moment before he pulled away. "So who are these other guys you're going out with?"

"Just guys from the area—not from town but not too far away. One is in real estate, and the other has done a lot of work in DC."

His lip curled up slightly. "Sounds great."

"I thought you were going to be encouraging. I don't have very long before Tori's wedding."

His expression smoothed out intentionally, as if he were making an effort to do so. "I know. I'm sure your other dates will be fine."

"I hope they're better than fine."

"So bo-ring," Beau squawked.

Jace chuckled. "That would be my prediction."

She gave him a friendly swat and then slid off the jacket she still wore. "Were you planning to go to bed? We could watch TV or something."

Jace started to answer. She saw his mouth open. But then he froze as he stared at her speechlessly, his eyes running up and down her body.

She glanced down. "What?" Self-conscious at his fixed gaze, she smoothed down her little blue dress. She'd made an effort at dressing this evening, and she'd thought the result was pretty and sexy.

Jace just stared, his body completely motionless.

"What?" she demanded again. "Is something wrong?"

"No," he managed to say hoarsely. "No." He looked away from her. "You look great."

She smiled at the compliment but said, "Well, you don't have to be all shocked about it. I can occasionally look good, you know."

"I know," Jace muttered, heading toward the living room to turn on the television. "Believe me, I know."

"So bo-ring," Beau chimed in.

The following night, Isabella was once again pounding on Jace's door.

This time, it was only ten o'clock, so she was surprised when Jace didn't come to the door immediately.

She knocked again and waited, wondering if Jace was out.

Irrationally, she didn't like that idea. What if he was on a date? Surely he would have told her if he'd been going out tonight.

She didn't like for him to keep secrets from her.

Where the hell was he?

She knocked again.

Finally, she heard some movement inside the apartment, and then Jace swung open the door.

His hair was damp, and he was wearing nothing but a pair of black sweatpants.

Her eyes widened at the sight of his fine shoulders and bare chest. He'd been very skinny in high school, but now he had a very nice, tight body, and she felt a moment of physical response to the sight of it.

"Is everything all right?" he asked, when she didn't say anything.

"Yes," she said, pushing through the tension in her

throat and tearing her eyes away. "Sorry. Was I interrupting something?"

"No. I was just in the shower." He let her in, and she had to exert a ridiculous amount of effort not to leer at him.

What was wrong with her? It was just Jace. Her best friend for so long.

"Another boring date?" Jace asked as she slid off her jacket and slouched down onto the couch.

"So bo-ring."

Isabella looked to the corner of the room, where Beau was perched on the swing in his big cage. "Why is he locked up?"

"He pooped on my table," Jace said with a sneer at the bird.

Laughing, she got up and opened the door to the cage. "That mean Jace put you in prison for a natural bodily function. He's not very nice."

"That bird can keep his natural bodily functions to himself."

"So bo-ring," Beau squawked hopefully, flying over to perch on the back of a dining room chair.

"We've got to teach you something else to say." Isabella said, going to get some grapes from the refrigerator. "Can you say, 'Hi, Bella'?"

"So bo-ring."

She kept the grape out of range of Beau's beak. "Hi, Bella."

"Hi-li."

This was at least an attempt so she gave the bird a grape. "Hi, Bella," she said very slowly. "Hi, Bella."

"Hi, Be-li. Hi, Be-li."

She laughed and rewarded this performance with more grapes. Then turned back to Jace, who was pulling on a T-shirt. "He's super smart. I didn't think parrots learned words that quickly."

"Oh, he's an evil genius, all right. I had to put a towel over his cage last night because he wouldn't stop screaming about how boring everything was." His eyes narrowed as she kept giggling. "Sure, you can laugh. You're not the one who has to live with the feathered freak."

When they'd both sat down on the couch, he turned to her and said, "So what was wrong with this date?"

"What makes you think something was wrong with it?"

"You're over here at ten o'clock. Obviously it wasn't a winner."

She sighed, thinking back to dinner she'd just had with another guy from the dating site. "He was an asshole."

Jace's shoulders stiffened slightly. "What did he do?"

"He didn't do anything. He just talked about himself the whole time. I've never met someone so pumped up on his own importance. I had to hear all about his car and his apartment and all the people he knows in DC. Ugh. He didn't ask me a single thing about myself, and then he thought I was going to invite him back to my place afterward."

"I hope you let him have it."

"Well, I might have mentioned that I'm not inclined to invite arrogant assholes back to my apartment."

Jace chuckled appreciatively. "Good for you."

Her eyes rested on his face for a minute, wondering why she all of a sudden found him so attractive. It must have something to do with her reaction to going out with two losers in a row. She'd always found Jace very cute— even way back in high school. But she'd never been distracted by it like this before.

"What?" he asked, his turning his head as if he'd felt her staring.

"What what?"

"Why are you looking at me like that?"

"I wasn't. I was just glad to be with a nice guy after that nightmare of a date."

"Maybe you should give up and cancel your date on Friday."

"I'm not going to give up. Surely there's a decent guy in the area who is still single."

"Right," Jace muttered. "A decent guy who is still single."

Something in his tone made her reach out and put a hand on his arm. "Other than you, I mean. You're the most decent guy I know."

He smiled and rolled his eyes slightly. "Did you want to stay and watch TV?"

"Sure. Why not? Nothing better to do tonight."

~

The following Friday, Isabella was knocking on Jace's door again, more flustered and upset than she'd been the previous weekend.

If Jace wasn't here tonight, she was definitely going to burst into tears.

She sighed in relief when he swung open the door, wearing his normal sweats and a T-shirt with a frog in a crown on it she'd bought for him last year.

Instead of his normal greeting, he studied her face for a minute and pulled her inside. "What happened?" he asked urgently. "Bella, what happened?"

"Nothing," she managed to say, more emotional because of his obvious concern.

"Something is wrong. What happened on your date?"

She took a few breaths and managed to control herself. "It's really nothing major. He was another jerk."

"What did he do?" Jace was still eyeing her urgently, as if searching for signs of damage.

"He was okay during dinner, but then we took a walk and he turned into Mr. McGropey."

"*What*?" Jace demanded, his whole body tensing.

"He was really gropey. It was... humiliating and disgusting." When she saw his expression, she hurried on. "It wasn't a huge deal though. He didn't force himself on me. He just groped when it was way too soon. I mean, we were in public, so I just pushed him away and went back to my car. But the whole thing made me feel dirty."

"Who is this guy?" Jace growled, his hands clenched at his sides.

"Just a guy."

"Tell me who he is."

"So you can go beat him up or something? Don't be ridiculous. It was... yuck, but it's over. I want to just forget about it."

"I want to know who he—"

"Jace, would you stop? I didn't come over here so you could save me. I just wanted... wanted..." She trailed off, her throat tightening again.

Jace's expression changed. "Oh, I'm sorry, Bella. Come here." He pulled her into a tight hug.

She shook against him for a minute, feeling better, loved, known.

When she finally pulled away, Jace asked, "You want to watch a movie?"

"Yeah. Thanks."

He got them beers and then settled on the couch to watch a light romantic comedy—which he let her pick out. He even put his arm around her so she could snuggle up against him.

She felt a lot better when the movie finished and she got up to leave.

"You can stay if you need to," Jace said, looking rumpled and concerned and adorable.

"I'm fine." She leaned over to kiss him on the cheek. "Thank you."

"You're welcome. Call me when you get home."

She laughed. "I will." Then she suddenly remembered

something. "Hey, where's Beau? I thought Erin wasn't going to be back for a couple of weeks?"

"She's not. Beau is finally sleeping after driving me crazy all evening. Don't you dare wake him up." Jace gestured over toward the bird cage which was covered with a blanket. Isabella had been so distracted she hadn't even noticed it before.

"Okay." She smiled and kissed his cheek again. Then wondered why she was doing that.

She wasn't in the habit of kissing Jace. She must be feeling particularly vulnerable.

"I'll walk you to your car," Jace said as they closed the apartment door behind them.

They were passing the stairs that led down to the basement when an elderly woman with a head full of pink sponge curlers was coming up, carrying a small laundry basket.

"Good evening, young man," she said to Jace. Then she turned to Isabella. "And you too, young lady."

Isabella had been hanging around Jace's apartment building long enough to have met Estelle Berry, one of his upstairs neighbors, on multiple occasions.

"Hi, Mrs. Berry," she said with a smile.

"Isn't it kind of late to have company?" Estelle asked, frowning disapprovingly at Jace.

"I'd just stopped by after a bad date," Isabella explained, not wanting Jace to get the reputation of being a scoundrel with his old-fashioned neighbor.

NOELLE ADAMS & SAMANTHA CHASE

Estelle's sharp eyes moved between her face and Jace's, as if she were coming to some sort of conclusion Isabella didn't understand. Then she gave a little smile. "I see. Well, it's fortunate I ran into you. My friend Gladys has a neighbor who is a fine young man and is recently divorced, so he's on the market again. He would be a perfect match for you, young lady."

Isabella blinked in surprise, while Jace tensed slightly beside her.

"Really?" Isabella asked.

"Yes. Shall I tell him you're interested?"

"I don't know. I'd have to know more about him."

"Excellent. I'll arrange it. He's a fine young man, and it's long past time for you to settle down."

As if the matter was completely decided, Estelle started walking with her laundry basket up the stairs to the second floor.

Both Isabella and Jace stared after her speechlessly.

"I can't believe she wants to set me up," Isabella breathed.

"You don't have to go out with the guy. He's probably an idiot if Estelle is trying to arrange it. You probably want to take a break from dating after tonight."

"No, I really don't. I'm still committed to finding someone by Tori's wedding. If someone wants to fix me up, then why shouldn't I consider it?" She paused, thinking through the possibilities. "Actually, it might be better to do it this way. Maybe I'll ask everyone I know to try to set me up with guys they know. I'll probably end up with better choices if people I know can vouch for them."

Jace stared at her, his lips parted slightly.

"What's wrong?" Isabella asked. "It's not that much different from using a dating site—I'll just have a layer of accountability." She nodded, pleased with this plan. "That's what I'm going to do."

"Oh. Okay."

"I thought you were going to be encouraging."

"Right. Encouraging."

She took his arm as they headed to the car. "If you were smart, you'd have your friends start to set you up on dates too."

He just grumbled in response, and Isabella was irrationally pleased by his reaction.

She knew it was wrong, but she didn't want people to start setting Jace up on dates.

She didn't like that idea at all.

4

DON'T BE BORING.

Don't be bragging.

Don't be gropey.

Jace looked at the column he'd listed as *don'ts* and felt fairly confident that he would not fall into any of those categories. For starters, he was a complete gentleman. There was no way he'd put his hands on a woman unless it was by mutual agreement. He certainly wasn't a braggart. If anything, he tended to want to talk about anything *but* himself. And although he wasn't the most interesting man in the world, he knew how to have a conversation where he was an active—and interesting—participant.

"Okay, so I'm good there."

For the next few minutes, he typed up all the information into a spreadsheet so he could try to find the exact combination of what he needed to become Isabella's perfect man. For a week he had been listening to her complain about the guys she had gone out with—he had been her shoulder to cry and complain on—and even though he had thought that he knew Isabella well, obviously it wasn't as well as he'd led himself to believe.

On the surface, Jace almost wanted to say that she was being overly picky. After all, what was she expecting on a first date? All first dates were awkward, but after listening to her talk about hers, they did all seem to have a rather high level of dysfunction. Bordering on creepiness.

"Don't be creepy," he said and added it to the list.

Jace would like to be perfect for Isabella, but even he knew that he had flaws. Plenty of them. But if he could get enough data on everything she was looking for, he could narrow the playing field in his favor and push his faults aside—suppress them, if you will—and hopefully make her fall in love with him.

With a sigh, he hung his head. "Pathetic. I'm getting totally pathetic."

"Pa-thetic," Beau mimicked.

Jace groaned.

Great. The last thing he needed right now was the damn bird mocking him again. He found himself talking to the bird a lot. Why couldn't the bird pick up on something nice or funny he'd said? Like last night, he'd watched a hockey game, and the Rangers had won. Did the damn bird remember his "Rangers Rule" chant? No. Of course not.

Birds were stupid.

It wasn't until he said that out loud and Beau repeated

it that Jace knew he couldn't take much more. So he got up and placed the cover over the cage to shut the little guy up. It was late enough to technically say it was his bedtime so no guilt.

Like that's completely normal—guilt over lying to a bird about its bedtime. I'm seriously losing my mind. He sat back down in front of his computer.

It was madness. He knew it was. And unhealthy. For him and for Isabella. If he could just get up the nerve to tell her how he felt, it would save them both so much time and energy. But she meant so much to him that he was afraid of saying or doing anything to ruin their relationship. And if she had given him even the slightest hint that she was interested, he might reconsider doing all this covert research.

But she hadn't.

If anything, her behavior had gotten more confusing.

The hugging. The sudden kissing thing she was doing whenever she was getting ready to leave. What the hell was up with that? If he didn't know any better, he'd swear she was torturing him on purpose. Then he immediately rejected that thought because Isabella didn't have a mean bone in her body.

Oh God. Don't start thinking about her body. Just like that, an image of her came to mind.

Damn blue dress.

He hadn't meant to say it out loud, and he'd thought he was in the clear since the bird was covered up for the night. But Beau squawked something about a blue dress.

"You're supposed to be asleep under there!" he muttered and then groaned. This was his pathetic life—dreaming about a woman who he desperately wanted and admonishing a bird who he desperately wanted to leave. And on top of that, now he was thinking about that dress after he had been trying so hard to forget it!

Yeah, that image had been playing on a continuous loop in his head for days. The only thing that stopped it was the reminder of their last conversation and her new plan to let people set her up. Besides Estelle's lead on a date, Jace had no doubt it would only be a matter of time before people around Preston got wind of it and started finding guys for her to go out with. Then what? What was he supposed to do if she got set up with someone he knew? How the hell was he supposed to handle that?

Just the thought of it made his head hurt. A lot of his friends were already married or at least in committed relationships, but he did know a few guys that would probably love a chance to go out with someone like Isabella. With a huff, he pulled up another blank document and started making a list of all the guys he knew and what he thought they'd have in common with her.

By the fourth name, Jace resigned himself to a late night and got up to make himself some coffee.

Three days later, his worst fears were confirmed.

There was everything except flyers being put up

around town to announce that Isabella was looking for a nice guy to settle down with. Everywhere he went, it was all people were talking about, and even at work, guys were approaching him asking for advice on how to approach her!

What the hell?

As he made his way across the street to Isabella's salon, he did his best to give himself a mental pep talk so that he didn't come off as an overprotective or jealous jerk when he saw her.

As he pulled the door open, he knew he was going to be hard pressed to pull that off.

"So my nephew Joe—"

"No, no, no! You don't want to go out with him. My Martin would be perfect—"

"Martin came out last year, Gloria! Stop trying to change the boy—"

"What about Derek the cop? Has anyone thrown him in the hat?"

There were a half a dozen women in the salon, and they were all talking at once. Jace caught Isabella's eye in the mirror and saw her look of amusement. At least one of them was having fun with this, he thought.

"Oh, Jace! Good. Maybe you can get this girl to see reason," Mrs. Pendergast called out. "Tell Isabella that my son Adam would be a perfect match for her. He's an accountant, and he loves kids and animals, and he's looking to settle down. And he definitely would love to settle down with a hometown girl."

Jace had to hide his smirk. He knew Adam Pendergast. They'd known each other since elementary school when they'd played Little League together. It wasn't that Adam was a bad guy. He wasn't. But perfect for Isabella? Definitely not. And not just because Jace didn't want him to be. Adam was a large man.

A very large man.

A very large man who enjoyed sharing pictures of his cat.

While talking to people at Star Trek conventions.

Um, yeah. He was pretty sure he could cross Adam off the list of potential competitors.

"Isabella," Mrs. Pendergast started up again, "trust me. You won't find a finer man than Adam. And I just know you'll love Mr. Whiskers too. And when you see how sweet Adam is with him, you'll see that he'll make a good father one day too."

This time Jace had to cough to hide his laughter.

"Oh, Jace! Are you okay?" Isabella cried, but Jace knew she was reacting just to get away from the conversation. "Come on," she said, patting him on the back as he pretended to keep coughing. "I have some water in the back."

Together they crossed the room and went into the back storage area where they both broke out in a quiet fit of laughter.

"Oh my God!" she said quietly, even as she giggled. "It's been like this all day!"

"Have all the offers included examples of how having a

pet makes you a good parent?" he asked, trying to sound serious.

"Stop it," she replied, playfully smacking his arm. "What am I supposed to do? How do I get out of that?"

"Honestly? I have no idea. I mean I still can't believe how this thing has taken on a life of its own. Everyone in town is talking about finding you a husband, for crying out loud!" He instantly sobered because he realized how he was starting to sound like a disgruntled ex or something.

"It's not that bad." She walked over to the refrigerator and pulled out a bottle of water, handing it to him. "I mean it's bad but nothing I can't handle." She paced a little and then gasped and ran around and hid behind his back, grasping his arms like a lifeline.

He didn't have to ask.

He knew the drill.

"You guys should just get an exterminator in here," he said, looking down and spotting the spider scurrying across the floor.

"Less talking, more stomping!" she said fiercely.

So he did what he had to do and then cleaned up the evidence. Turning around, he faced her with a smile. "There. Happy?"

She seemed to visibly relax, a serene smile on her face. "My hero. What would I do without you?"

He had the perfect opening there for all the reasons he was the right guy for her and how they'd be perfect for each other.

"Bella? Is everything all right back there? I think Mrs.

Pendergast is ready to go!" Elise called back to her.

That brought Jace's ponderings to an abrupt halt. "So what are you going to tell Mrs. Pendergast?"

She sighed. "I don't know. I just have to comb her out, ring her up, and get her out of here. If I can keep her distracted while I do it, maybe we can just pretend those last few minutes never happened."

Jace wasn't convinced. "When was the last time that woman left here without getting the last word on something?"

Isabella's shoulders sagged. "Damn. I really don't want to hurt her feelings."

"You could just tell her that you've changed your mind. Or that you've already found the perfect guy."

She frowned at him. "I'm not going to lie to her, Jace. That's not nice either. She's a sweet woman and a good customer. And besides, if I said I found the perfect guy, she'll want to know who it is. Then what do I say?"

He shrugged and decided to throw it out there—lightly —and see how she responded.

"Me. Tell her it's me," he said casually. "Tell her that we decided to give this whole dating thing a try."

For a moment, Isabella didn't move. Didn't blink.

Oh God. Was she disgusted? Horrified?

Then she burst out laughing.

Hard.

Like bending in two because of all the laughing.

Jace didn't take that as a good sign.

When she straightened, she looked at him and reached

out to squeeze his shoulder. "Oh my goodness! Could you imagine? That might be a great temporary distraction, but she'd see through it in a hot second!" She wiped away tears of mirth and then checked her reflection in the small mirror on the wall. "But thanks for making me laugh. I've got to get back out there and ring her up. Feel free to come out when the coast is clear."

And then she was gone.

And Jace was left standing there wondering what his next move was supposed to be.

Just when he thought things couldn't get any worse, they did.

Isabella had invited him to lunch, and at first he had taken it as a good thing, but then she added, "I need to get some info on a guy from you. Can you meet me for pizza at one?"

"Yeah," he said wearily. "Sure."

At lunch, they ordered and grabbed a booth. No sooner had he taken his jacket off than she was firing questions at him.

"So my friend Julie set me up with her cousin Greg, who works for the town. Do you know him? Greg Channing?"

He nodded and took a bite of his pizza.

"Well? What's he like? Is he cute? Is he nice? Am I going to have anything in common with him?" She sighed.

"Is it crazy that I'm going out on a blind date like this again?"

His immediate answer was yes, but he kept that to himself. With a shrug he said, "This is what you wanted to do, so..."

"Okay, you're right. You're right. So? Tell me something about him?"

"I don't know him all that well."

Lie number one.

He and Greg had worked together on several projects, played poker together on numerous occasions, and talked almost daily.

"Oh, come on. You have to know something about him," she prompted, picking up her own pizza as she looked at him expectantly.

"Well... uh. I have no idea what I'm supposed to say here."

"Is he good-looking?"

"I guess."

She sighed and shook her head. "Fine. Is he funny? Does he have a good sense of humor?"

"He does."

Lie number two.

Greg had a really weird sense of humor. Very dry. Very analytical. It was the type of humor he and Isabella normally mocked.

"Oh. Good," she said with relief. "Does he have any interests?"

Politics. The guy loved to talk about politics. Another

topic that he knew Isabella shied about from. "Current events. He's a good one to talk to about what's going on around town and that kind of thing."

Lie number three.

If she brought up anything local, Greg was likely to turn it into a political discussion. And no doubt, that was going to frustrate her to no end.

Hmm...

"I bet if you talked to him about some of the town stuff —the things you like about Preston and all that—you'd end up having a great conversation."

That seemed to please her even more. "Wow! Okay, great! I love that!" She took another bite of her pizza and after a minute asked, "So you think he's a good guy, right?"

"Absolutely."

A good guy to prove that you *shouldn't* be set up on dates.

Later that afternoon, Greg came into his office. "Hey, Jace. You got a minute?"

Looking up, he nodded. "Sure. What's up?"

"You're tight with Isabella Warner, right?"

Oh, for the love of... "Um, yeah. Why?"

"I'm taking her out tomorrow night. She's friends with my cousin Julie, and well, you know. So I don't know her all that well, but I figured since you do, you could sort of give me some tips so that I don't mess things up."

Remembering his earlier conversation with Isabella, Jace figured this was his perfect opportunity to make sure this date was of the one-and-only-one variety.

"Sure. What would you like to know?"

"Well, what is she interested in? What kind of topics should I avoid?" Greg asked.

"Isabella loves to talk about politics! I think the two of you are going to have some lively conversation on that topic. She's heavily invested in the political workings of Preston, so you're gold there."

"Really? Okay, that's awesome! What else?"

"Let's see. She loves a good sense of humor. But the mature kind. Nothing overly silly or anything like that. I'll bet if you even pulled out some of those jokes and commentaries about the election, she'll enjoy them."

"Wow, so she is really into politics, huh?"

"You have no idea," Jace said with a small grin.

"And where does she like to eat? She told me to pick a place and just text her and let her know, but I'd love to pick a place that she'd like."

This could really put a final nail in this date's coffin, but Jace figured he was doing this for all the right reasons so...

"Thai food. She loves it!"

She hated it.

With a passion.

"Oh, that's perfect! It's my favorite too." He smiled and sank down in the chair opposite Jace's desk. "I really appreciate the help, Jace. From everything Julie's told me,

Isabella sounds like an amazing woman. I don't want to do anything to mess up. You know how awkward first dates can be."

"I certainly do," Jace said cryptically.

"Anyway, I can't even remember the last time I was set up on a date. Joanne and I were together for six years, and ever since the divorce... well... I haven't really been comfortable with the thought of dating. I mean, Joanne and I were high school sweethearts. So she's the only woman I ever... you know."

Oh good Lord. TMI!

"You should be honest with Isabella. Tell her that. I'm sure if she knows how nervous you are about this being your first time out since the divorce, it will go a long way in relaxing her."

"You think so?"

"Sure."

He had no idea. All he knew was that if he was out on a date with a woman who admitted to never having been on a date with anyone but her ex, he'd be majorly uncomfortable. He only hoped that Isabella felt the same way.

Greg looked at his watch and stood. "I need to get back to it. Thanks again for the advice, Jace. You're a good friend."

He wasn't so sure about that. What he was was desperate.

"No problem, Greg. Good luck and have a good weekend!"

5

ISABELLA'S EYES GLAZED OVER AS GREG LAUNCHED INTO another endless diatribe about exactly what was wrong with DC politics.

She was only mildly interested in politics in the best of times, and this kind of useless discoursing always drove her crazy.

Everyone seemed to want to fix politics by talking about it. Very few people wanted to get involved and actually *work* at it. Greg was clearly no exception.

She tried to smile and nod politely, glad at least she didn't have to participate in the conversation any more than humming encouragingly every once in a while. She didn't understand why more guys couldn't be like Jace— who always asked her questions, listened when she spoke, wanted to hear what she had to say.

It had been fifty minutes now since they'd sat down at this table in a Thai restaurant in the town over from

Preston. She hated Thai food, so that was a bad sign from the very beginning. Fortunately, she'd suggested they meet here, so as soon as dinner was over, she could get into her car and escape.

"Oh," Greg said, evidently noticing at last that she was amusing herself looking at other diners in the restaurant. "I've been doing all the talking. What do you think?"

What did she think? About what exactly? About anything in the world?

That was as useless a question as "how are you?"

"I agree with you," she said with a little smile, deciding that was easier than making any sort of claim that could encourage him to launch into another political rant. "It's too bad everyone doesn't agree."

He smiled, as if she'd said exactly the right thing, and she tried not to roll her eyes.

He seemed a nice enough guy, and he was decent-looking. If he didn't feel obliged to fill every moment of the conversation with political talk, she might actually like him.

"Do you want dessert?" he asked.

"No, thank you. I'm really full. This was delicious." She pushed her mostly empty plate to the side in a clear gesture that she was finished.

"Oh. What about some more wine?"

"No, thank you. I've had enough since I'll need to drive home."

"I can drive you ho—"

"No, no. I'm fine. Thank you."

Greg sighed, his shoulders slumping. "That doesn't sound very promising. Have I made a mess of the date then?"

She suddenly felt bad for her attitude. It wasn't Greg's fault he was boring as hell, and she didn't like hurting anyone's feelings. "No, no. It's not that. I guess I'm just kind of tired tonight. You seem like a really nice guy."

"Thanks." He gave a huff of amusement. "No need to sugarcoat it. If you don't like me, you don't like me. The truth is I haven't had much experience in dating."

"Really?" She was surprised and genuinely interested, since men didn't usually talk like that on dates.

"Yeah. I've only ever dated one woman seriously. My ex. I'm... I haven't gotten around much."

From his tone, she suddenly realized what he was talking about. Not just about dating. He was implying he'd only ever slept with one woman.

The strangest thing was she liked him better now than she had before. It felt like he was being real, being honest.

She liked that trait in a man.

"Well, that's okay. It's not like I've been a social butterfly or anything. Everyone has different experiences."

"So you don't think it's weird or... or pitiful?"

"Why would it be pitiful?" she asked. "I actually think it's kind of nice—that you take relationships seriously, I mean."

He smiled at her, and she smiled back.

She still wasn't really attracted to him, and she didn't think there was much potential after the tedious dinner they'd just had, but she felt better about him now. She liked him as a person. She was glad to have met him.

"So you might consider going out with me again?"

"Maybe," she said, not wanting to trap herself by being too nice. "I mean, maybe something friendly and casual. Just as long as you don't spend the whole time talking about politics."

He blinked in surprise and then smiled. "It's a deal."

Since their dinner ended early, it was just nine o'clock when Isabella drove back to Preston. By instinct, she steered her car toward Jace's apartment building.

When she saw his car in its place, she parked in a visitor space and got out.

Her first instinct was always to go see Jace, whenever anything noteworthy happened to her—even a very strange date.

It occurred to her as she was walking toward the building that things would have to change between her and Jace when one or the other of them finally was in a serious relationship. They couldn't keep hanging out together all the time the way they did now. No one would be okay with their significant other spending so much time with someone else of the opposite sex.

It was inevitable, natural. Isabella had always known it would happen.

But the thought of it right now caused a sudden stab of pain to shoot through her chest.

She would hate not to be able to hang out with Jace all the time, tell him all her thoughts and feelings, hear his opinions and complaints and encouragements.

A life without Jace in it that way felt sterile and empty.

"Isabella," a voice came from behind her, startling her out of her bleak reverie.

She turned around to see Heather Carver, a small, pretty blonde she'd gone to high school with. Heather lived in an apartment in Preston's Mill too—in fact, her father's company had restored the old mill and converted it into apartments.

"Hi, Heather," she said with a smile as the other woman approached. "How's everything going?"

"Good, good!" Heather flashed her a beaming smile. "You heard Chris and I are engaged, didn't you?"

"Of course I heard. I work in the beauty salon, remember. I'm so happy for you. When is the wedding?"

"We're still working on setting the date." The two women walked up the front steps. "Are you here to visit Jace?"

"Yes. Who else?"

Heather chuckled. "Are you two still just friends or have things moved along to something more?"

Isabella blinked in surprise and stopped walking. "Of course we're just friends. There's never been anything else between us."

"Sometimes that changes though. Right?"

"I... guess." Isabella felt a weird twisting in her stomach she'd felt occasionally in the past, whenever the nature of her friendship with Jace was analyzed. She didn't like for people to question them. Sometimes it felt like everyone else was skeptical that a friendship like hers and Jace's could even exist. "But ours won't change. We've been friends like this since high school."

"And neither of you ever considered something more than friendship?" Heather wasn't being rude, although a little smile played on the corners of her mouth. She seemed genuinely interested, and she'd always been sweet and friendly with Isabella.

Isabella shook her head. "No. I was dating Brock when Jace and I started hanging out back in high school. So anything more than friendship was out of the question. I was with Brock for so long that our relationship just got established as friendship. If it hasn't changed yet, I don't think it's ever going to change. Is that so strange?"

"I don't know. Maybe not. But Brock is out of the picture now, isn't he?"

"Yes. He's long gone. And honestly it feels like I wasted a lot of my life on him. But I wouldn't have become friends with Jace if I hadn't been going out with Brock, so I can't regret it."

"Jace is pretty cute, you know."

Isabella stiffened. Her first instinct—ridiculously—had been a stab of jealousy that any other woman was thinking Jace was cute. Heather was engaged though, and Isabella had no call to be jealous of anyone. She let out a breath and let go of the silly feeling. "I know he's cute."

"So maybe don't take something more than friendship off the table completely. You never know."

"Right," Isabella said with a slightly forced smile. "You never know."

She agreed mostly to end the conversation. She was feeling that twisting in her stomach again. She hated that feeling.

"Sorry," Heather said, obviously reading something on Isabella's face. "It's none of my business. I hope I didn't annoy you too much."

"No, not at all." Isabella's smile was real this time, relieved that part of the conversation was over. "I'm glad I ran into you, actually. We should hang out some time."

"Definitely. Give me a call, and we'll set something up."

So the two were on good terms when they said good-bye. Heather started up the stairs to her and Chris's apartment on the second floor, and Isabella walked down the hall to Jace's apartment on the first floor.

She knocked on the door and waited until Jace unlocked the door and swung it open.

He wore jeans and another T-shirt she'd given him—this one with a big dog wearing a top hat on the front. He was always such a good sport about the silly shirts she gave him.

Her heart clenched unexpectedly as she saw him, his hair rumpled, his eyes slightly heavy behind his glasses, wearing the shirt she'd picked out for him. It was the strangest, most unexpected feeling of possession.

Like he was hers.

Like he belonged to her.

"What's the matter?" he asked, his eyebrows drawing together.

She swallowed, shaking herself out of the bizarre feeling. Clearly her conversation with Heather had rattled her more than it should have. "Nothing. Sorry. It's nothing."

"Another bad date?"

"It was... strange." She stared at him for a minute, waiting for him to step aside. Then finally she asked, "Can I come in?"

"Of course," he said, blinking as if he too had been in a strange daze. "Sorry. I'm just kind of out of it tonight, I guess."

She walked in and had a brief conversation with Beau, who squawked to her a few times a combination of "So boring" and "Hi, Bel-li" as she gave him a few grapes.

When the greetings were over, Jace went to get a couple of beers and Isabella collapsed onto his couch.

"So tell me about the date," Jace said, stretching his legs out and taking his glasses off.

"Most of it was terrible. He talked about politics the whole time. I was about to go out of my mind." She smiled. "But at the end we actually had a decent conversation."

Jace frowned. "About what?"

"About relationships. You know, he's only been with one other woman. Ever. Can you believe that?"

Jace made a noncommittal sound.

"Don't tell him I told you that. He'd probably be embarrassed. But it was actually kind of nice, that he was honest about it"

"It doesn't kind of freak you out?"

"Why would it? I'm not looking for some sort of player, you know." She gave him a teasing poke in the ribs. "And who are you to talk, anyway?"

His frown deepened. "I've been with more than one woman."

"I know you have. You're, what, up to three now?"

His eyes narrowed.

She giggled. "Is my count wrong?"

"Yes, your count is wrong."

"So what's the number then?" She and Jace didn't normally talk about sex. In fact, that had an unspoken rule not to bring it up. She wasn't sure why she was pushing the issue now. She just couldn't help it.

He kept frowning and didn't reply.

"Tell me! I'll tell you. I'm at four."

He sighed, his expression relaxing. "I'm at four too."

She giggled again and leaned over to kiss his jaw. "We match! I always knew we were a good pair."

She was pulling away from the kiss when he turned his head, and suddenly their lips were only an inch apart.

Her breath caught in her throat as she had to fight the desire to kiss his mouth.

What the hell was wrong with her? She was never like this. Not with Jace. This was completely inappropriate.

She straightened up quickly and leaned back against the couch, putting distance between their lips again.

Jace cleared his throat and shifted, as if he were uncomfortable. "So how did you leave it with Greg?"

"He wants to go out again, and I said maybe something casual. As long as he doesn't talk endlessly about politics. Why do guys do that? Is it supposed to impress us?"

"I have no idea." He cleared his throat again and then took a long swig of beer. "You want to watch a movie or something?"

"Sure." She toed off her shoes and folded her legs up onto the couch to get more comfortable. "What were you doing this evening?"

"Just catching up on some work."

"Why are you working on a Friday night?"

He gave a shrug. "Figured I'd just get it done."

"You don't want to go out on dates too?"

"Who would I go out with?"

"I'm sure we could find you someone. What about—"

"Please don't try to set me up."

Isabella blinked at his tone, which was almost bad-tempered. "I'm sorry. I was just trying to help."

"I know. But I'm fine. I don't need to be set up. If I want to go out, I can find someone. I'm not a total loser, you know."

"I know. You're smart and funny and cute and sexy. Women should be pounding down your door. I really don't know why they're not." Her cheeks flushed slightly as she realized what she'd said.

Had she actually said that Jace was sexy?

What was wrong with her tonight?

He gave her a little smile, but his eyes were soft, almost tender. "Thanks."

They stared at each other for a minute until Jace evidently remembered he was supposed to be finding a movie for them to watch.

They picked out an old action film that both of them liked and settled in to watch it.

After about fifteen minutes, Isabella started to get cold, so she reached over Jace's body to grab a blanket from the other side of the couch.

"Help yourself," he teased. "Don't mind me sitting here."

She laughed and spread the blanket out over her. "Are you cold too?"

"Not really."

"We can share."

"I'm really fine."

Despite his words, his expression was fond and laughing, and she couldn't seem to resist it tonight. She wanted to be close to him.

She rearranged the blanket so it was covering him too, and then she cuddled up against him.

He put his arm around her, and she liked how it felt. A lot.

He made her feel like she was protected, known, cherished.

Taken care of.

They watched the movie together like that, and when it ended she knew she needed to pull away. She was feeling far too affectionate, far too close to him.

Their relationship was too good and special for something weird to get between them.

She couldn't let things get weird.

But she also couldn't seem to pull away, and he didn't appear inclined to remove his arm from around her.

With his free hand, he clicked the remote, looking for something else to watch.

"I guess I should go home," she said since it felt like something she was supposed to say.

"No hurry."

"Just tell me when you're ready for me to leave."

"I'm never ready for you to leave, Bella."

Her breath hitched at the words, and she was too nervous to look at his face to see his expression.

"Remember back in high school when I stayed half the night playing video games at your place, and Brock showed up all mad about it?"

Jace chuckled, still flipping channels. "Of course I remember. He said that obviously nothing would happen between us, but you were still his girlfriend and he didn't like it."

Isabella shook her head. "He was always kind of jealous of us, I think."

"He was."

"I think maybe he knew deep down that we were closer than he and I ever were."

"Yeah."

She felt that twisting in her stomach again, the one that made her so uncomfortable. "Sometimes I worry," she admitted.

"About what?"

"About what will happen when I get a real boyfriend. Will he always be kind of jealous of you and me because we're so close?"

Jace moved his hand to stroke her hair gently and didn't answer.

"Do you ever worry about that?" she asked.

"Sometimes."

"What are we going to do?" Her voice wobbled slightly because the idea of pulling back from Jace was absolutely heartbreaking.

He sighed and stroked her hair again. "We'll figure it out."

"I don't want to lose you."

"You're not going to lose me. This I promise you."

She relaxed and snuggled against his warm body, pulling the blanket back up to her shoulders. She believed Jace. It sounded like he meant it.

He was smart. If both of them were committed to this friendship, then they would be able to work things out, even if one or both of them started a romantic relationship.

Things would be okay.

They had to be.

Her world wouldn't be right unless Jace was in it.

Jace settled on a cable channel that ran old sitcoms, and they watched them for a while.

Eventually Isabella's eyes grew heavy. She knew it was time for her to go home. She couldn't sleep on the couch like this with Jace.

But she didn't want to move. She didn't want to pull away from him.

So she stayed wrapped up in his arms, in the blanket, until she finally drifted off to sleep.

6

JACE WOKE UP, BUT HE WAS SURE HE WAS DREAMING.

Isabella was in his arms.

The last thing he remembered was them watching the TV with Isabella snuggling up beside him. Now they were lying down, a tangle of arms and legs and covered in a blanket.

It was amazing.

Doing his best to not wake her, he let himself indulge in the fantasy. Gently, one hand skimmed up her back and then into her hair while the other held her securely against him. With her head on his shoulder, he inhaled the floral scent of her shampoo before placing a light kiss on the top of her head.

A small groan escaped before he could help it.

This was torture.

Staring up at the ceiling, Jace mentally cursed himself. He had known that Isabella was falling asleep—knew there was a good chance of her not being able to drive home—and he hadn't done a thing about it. Now here he was, stuck in the most delicious form of hell, and it was all his own doing.

Idiot.

So what was he supposed to do? There was a good chance she'd be pissed when she woke up. Not that he'd done anything inappropriate—they were both fully clothed—but he couldn't help but worry that she would be upset with him for letting her fall asleep on his couch.

Okay, she'd done that a time or two in the past, but never for the whole night. So maybe rather than being upset, she'd be embarrassed that she'd done it. That he could work with. He could play it off like it wasn't any big deal and then move on.

Damn, but he was tired of moving on. Mainly because he wasn't. He was torturing himself because he was too afraid to do anything to rock the boat of this friendship. Something was going to have to give—soon—and he had a feeling this could be point of no return. It all depended on how Isabella reacted when she woke up in his arms.

He was making himself crazy with this inner conflict. So rather than continuing with speculating, Jace opted to return to the facts. *Fact*: they were best friends and had been for years. *Fact*: there wasn't anything he wouldn't do for her. *Fact*: he felt closer to her now more than ever—and not just because of their current position on the couch, but also because she was coming to him to share her thoughts and dreams on an almost daily basis.

It just sucked that those hopes and dreams related to the date she'd just been on.

Other men aside, it still had to mean something that after every date, she came to him. It could mean that she was willingly torturing him, but he quickly pushed that thought aside. Isabella didn't have a mean bone in her body, and she had no idea how her dating other guys was killing him. This whole dating experiment was important to her, and he was the one she kept sharing it with. Why? Because he meant something to her.

Now if only she would allow him to be more than a buddy, a pal, a... confidant.

Confidant wouldn't be bad—he could live with that—if it meant they were exclusive and romantically involved.

He groaned. God, he was sounding pathetic even inside his own head! What was it going to take to get him to...

Beside him, Isabella stretched and let out a very sexy sounding moan.

And if he wasn't already turned on, that little sound definitely would have done it.

He only prayed that she wasn't aware of just *how* turned on he was. Although, with her thigh precariously close to his straining erection, it was only a matter of time.

Great.

"Mmm, Jace." She sighed, and everything in him went still. Was she saying his name because she had opened her eyes and saw him, or was she sighing his name because she was dreaming about him? Too afraid to move or speak,

NOELLE ADAMS & SAMANTHA CHASE

he waited. Isabella shifted against him, her knee gently nudging his arousal, and he almost bucked right off the couch. "Jace?" she asked sleepily.

He prayed his voice didn't crack like a hormonal teenage boy. "Hey, Sleeping Beauty," he said softly, thankful for how calm he actually sounded.

Isabella lifted her head and blinked at him, her eyes still heavy from sleep. "What... what time is it?"

Jace looked over at the wall clock and then back at her. "A little after six."

A soft gasp was her first response.

Then a loud yawn.

"Sorry." She relaxed against him. "I can't believe I fell asleep." Then she chuckled.

"What? What's so funny?" he asked softly.

She chuckled again. "I can't believe I fell asleep and kept you pinned on the couch so you couldn't go to bed."

Okay. He could work with that.

Hugging her closer, he said, "Well, it wasn't so bad. I got caught up in the TV, and then it just seemed like too much effort to get up and walk all the way to the bed." He gave a careless shrug. "It's not the first time I've fallen asleep in front of the TV."

"Mmm."

They lay in companionable silence. Jace was too afraid of breaking the mood to speak, and he figured Isabella was struggling with maybe a gracious way to get up. Hell, if it were up to him, she could stay like this all day, and he would be perfectly content with that.

"Can I ask you something?" she finally said, as if following through on whatever she'd been thinking.

"Sure."

"I've been out on several dates already."

"Right."

"And there's one thing that worries me."

He let out a quiet, nervous laugh. "Just one?"

She laughed with him before going on. "Well, they've all been kind of disastrous and ended with me practically running for the door."

"And?"

Lifting her head, Isabella studied his face for a moment. "And not once did any of them kiss me goodnight."

Jace's heart hammered in his chest. Part of him was relieved by her declaration, and another part of him feared where she was going with this.

"Did you really want any of them to?" he asked after a minute.

She shook her head. "No, but it's kind of been a while and…"

"And?"

She let out a small huff. "Okay, don't laugh."

"Never."

"You know how you think you're a good kisser, but you never really know because it would be rude for someone to just come out and say you're a bad kisser?"

"Wait, who said I'm a bad kisser?" he asked in total confusion. How did they even get to this?

This laugh was bit throatier, and Isabella reached out and cupped his cheek. "Not you, silly. I'm saying that I always thought I was a decent kisser—Brock never complained—but we were so young when we dated, and then with the other guys... I don't know. It's been a while for me, and I'm sort of wondering what I'd do if one of these dates ended with a kiss."

"But that's how a date is supposed to end." He sat up and raked a hand through his hair with an edge of frustration. "Are you saying you don't want to kiss anyone goodnight?"

"You know what? Never mind," she sighed, lying back down.

"No. Come on. I'm still half asleep, and I guess I'm not following what you're talking about."

Another sigh. She looked up at him, and he could see the uncertainty in her eyes. "What if I'm not a good kisser? What if that ends up being a deal breaker? What if I'm throwing out some sort of vibe that makes guys not want to kiss me?"

Was she serious? Was this really a thing?

"Uh, Bella, are you crazy? Are you sure *you're* really awake? Because you're not making sense. Why would you even think such a thing about yourself?"

"It's not crazy to be insecure about certain things," she said stiffly, looking away from him. "I just want to find someone that I connect with and don't want to be the one to ruin it because, you know, I'm too nervous or uptight about my kissing skills."

If he was dreaming, he really wished he'd wake up right about now because this conversation was beyond bizarre.

"Bella, maybe—"

"Will you kiss me?" she said quickly.

"Uh, what?" There was no way he heard that right. No. Way.

"Would you kiss me?"

"Bella, I don't think..."

She sat up and looked him squarely in the eye, her expression pleading. "Jace, I trust you. There's no one in the world I trust more. So if we kiss and it's not good, you'd tell me. Right?"

"I don't think—"

Placing a finger over his lips, she stopped whatever he was going to say. Hell, even that small touch had him getting harder than he thought possible.

"I know it's not going to be great. I mean I know we're not attracted to each other that way, but I guess I'm asking if my... technique is okay. Does that make sense?"

None of this made sense, and he had to hold his tongue from saying that to her. She wanted him to kiss her? He would do it. And not because she was asking— although that in and of itself was an answer to a prayer— but because this was his chance to prove to her that he was more than just a guy who was her friend.

But what if *his* kissing technique sucked?

Oh, God. How did this get so complicated?

"You're thinking too hard about this," she said lightly.

NOELLE ADAMS & SAMANTHA CHASE

"This shouldn't be a big deal, right? We've shared just about everything else. How hard could this be?"

She had no idea.

"And I don't want you to feel bad about telling me if I'm not a good kisser. I really want to know, okay?"

"Bella, maybe... maybe..."

"Wouldn't you want to know if you were a bad kisser?"

Right now? No. Absolutely not.

There was no going back. He was going to kiss her, and Jace already knew there wasn't a chance in hell of her being a bad kisser. It was impossible. But if *he* was, he didn't want to know.

"Okay," he said after a minute. "But here's the thing, we're not critiquing *me*. This is about you." *Good save.* "I don't want you thinking about me." *Liar.* "Just focus on the kiss, okay?"

She nodded and then licked her lips.

Killing. Him. Slowly.

Isabella looked at him anxiously. Was he just supposed to swoop in and do it? Lean in slowly? Grab her?

As if reading his mind, she laughed softly. "I think we should just sort of pretend this is the end of a date and we're kissing goodnight. It would be a slow, sort of—"

She never got to finish.

Jace didn't want this to be a clinical play-by-play. He wanted *her*. He wanted to finally know what her lips felt like against his. Cupping her face, his lips claimed hers, and she completely melted against him.

Slowly, he pulled her to him until they were almost

back in the same position they had woken up in—except now she was almost sprawled out on top of him. One of his hands raked up into her hair, anchoring her to him, and Jace was aware of one of Isabella's hands doing the same to him.

Same. Page.

It didn't take long for the kiss to go from chaste to erotic. As soon as his tongue gently teased at her lips, she eagerly opened for him. And within a heartbeat, he went from kissing to being kissed. Hungrily.

Damn.

Isabella had some serious kissing skills.

And she was destroying him.

Over and over they came together—tongues dueling, lips claiming—and Jace didn't care if he never breathed again just as long as they kept doing this.

She shifted, straddled him, and he knew there was no way to disguise the effect she had on him. So he went with it—arching up slightly and rubbing against her—and was surprised when she moaned and did some rubbing and grinding of her own.

Was this it? Were they finally going to do this?

Lifting his lips from her, he trailed kisses along her jaw as he panted her name over and over.

"Jace, please," she gasped, pressing impossibly closer to him.

Flipping her over, he sprawled out on top of her and immediately claimed her lips again. God, she was so sweet, tasted so good. He wanted to kiss every inch of her. His hand left that glorious mane of hair and began to move—caressing her cheek, the slender column of her throat, until he finally cupped her breast.

Isabella tore her lips from his and purred his name.

Yes! Yes! Yes!

He knew they'd be good together. Knew that if she just gave him a chance he could prove to her...

"Oh my God!" She stiffened beneath him. But it wasn't the good *Oh my God* that he was hoping for. Nope. This was more like *What the hell have I done?*

Jace felt her slight shove and misjudged where he was. No sooner had she moved than he found himself face down on the floor as she stepped over him.

Wow. Never had a woman so disgusted by my kisses that they shoved me to the floor, was his first, irrational thought.

She was going to hate him. He'd gotten carried away, and now he'd ruined everything. With a sigh of defeat, he stayed in his position and waited.

"I am so sorry," she said, her face hidden behind her hands. "I... I don't even know what to say. That was... oh God."

Wait. She was apologizing?

Carefully, he turned his head to see her more clearly.

"Oh, God. Look what I did to you." She turned away.

It would have been great if she'd offered him a hand, but okay, fine. He could still look cool and collected as he scrambled to his feet.

Sort of.

"Bella," he said, standing up—and ignoring the tent of his sweatpants.

But she was walking toward the door to collect her purse and coat. "I... I don't even know what to say."

"Bella, talk to me," he pled, hurrying after her. Grasping her shoulders, he forced her to face him.

"I really need to go," she said but wouldn't look him in the eye. "That was... I mean... it was a stupid idea. I never should have asked."

"It wasn't a stupid idea," he argued, feeling more than a little annoyed at her response when just seconds ago, she was writhing in his arms and sighing his name. "There's nothing wrong with what just happened."

But she pulled away. "No, I... it was. I'm so sorry. It was my fault. And I need to go." Then she did meet his gaze. "Please."

And with that one devastated look, he stepped back and nodded. He would deny her nothing. Without another word, she opened the door and walked away, leaving him standing there wondering which of them she was really more upset with.

7

ISABELLA WAS SO FLUSTERED AND CONFUSED AS SHE LEFT Jace's apartment that she ended up driving aimlessly around town.

She didn't even know where to go.

Her phone rang once, and she knew it was Jace. She ignored the call and decided not to return to her own apartment since Jace might end up heading over there if he couldn't get her on the phone.

She didn't work until the afternoon, so after making a circuit around Preston three times, she finally ended up pulling into her parents' long driveway.

They lived in a comfortable brick ranch on the outskirts of town on a street with just three other houses on it. She'd lived in this house until she was eighteen. Every time she walked in, it felt like a warm hug—comforting, familiar, known.

She knew from the cars in the driveway that two of her

sisters, Tori and Carla, must be here. She headed toward the kitchen, where the family usually gathered.

Isabella stopped in the doorway when she saw that her mother was the only one in the kitchen and every surface was covered with baking apparatus.

"Hello, dear," her mother said, glancing up from the dough she was kneading. "I'm happy to see you, but don't you dare come in."

For her mother, baking was serious business, and any onlookers had the potential to sabotage the works. Isabella gave a faint smile, feeling better at this familiar warning. "I won't. I just stopped by to hang out."

"Tori and Carla are on the sunporch. I'll be done in about an hour."

"Okay. Thanks."

Isabella backed away from the kitchen and headed to the rear of the house, where she found two of her three sisters sitting on the old couch, peering at Tori's tablet.

Carla glanced up and smiled. "Tori is having trouble deciding on flowers for the wedding," she explained. "Come look at the options."

Pleased with the distraction, she came over and sat on Tori's other side, leaning over to get a better look at the possibilities.

Isabella had had the flowers for her wedding picked out since she was in junior high.

Not that she was any closer to getting married now than she'd been back then.

NOELLE ADAMS & SAMANTHA CHASE

Pushing away the feeling, she focused on the decision at hand. "I like them all."

"So do we." Tori sighed and leaned back. "I narrowed it down to the good ones, and now I just don't know. It would be nice if Jeff wanted to participate in the planning, but he has nothing to say but, 'Anything you want is fine with me.'"

Carla chuckled, and even Isabella smiled at her sister's aggrieved tone. "I guess a lot of guys don't really care that much about flower arrangements," she said. She turned to her other sister and asked, "Are you feeling any better?"

"Yes! I haven't thrown up in three days! Maybe this horrible endless morning sickness is finally over. I was afraid I'd be one of those women who have morning sickness for the entire pregnancy."

Isabella tried to smile and react appropriately to this comment, but she was suddenly hit with a wave of mortification and confusion, as she remembered kissing Jace.

What had she done?

She'd been so out of it this morning, not thinking clearly. Reflecting on how nice it felt to wake up with Jace and hoping she'd have a man to wake up with like that every morning.

But her brain clearly hadn't been working at full capacity for her to ask Jace to kiss her the way she had.

Had she destroyed so many years of friendship with a moment's stupidity?

"What's the matter?" Tori demanded, her eyes narrowing as she peered at Isabella's face.

"Nothing."

"Don't lie," Carla said. "You look weird. What's going on?"

"Nothing," Isabella tried again. Then she sighed and admitted, "I don't really know."

"It's not your date last night, is it?" Tori asked.

"No. No, nothing like that."

"Something with Jace then?" Tori had put down her tablet and was focusing completely on her sister.

Isabella's shoulders stiffened. "Why would you assume it has to do with Jace?"

Carla laughed softly. "Call it a lucky guess. Now what's going on?"

Fighting through her instinctive resistance at admitting how silly she'd been, she finally managed to say, "I... we... kissed."

Both her sisters sat up straight, their eyes wide.

Before they could give voice to their obvious surprise, Isabella hurried on. "It was... it was really stupid. Just a thing that happened. It wasn't supposed to be serious. But now it has me all confused and upset."

"What did he say?"

"Nothing. He... I didn't give him a chance to say anything. I just ran out of there."

"Well, that was dumb." Carla was giving a familiar big-sisterly frown of disapproval.

"I know, but I didn't know what to say. We've been friends for so long. That wasn't supposed to happen. And now it feels like everything has changed."

"Do you want it to change?" Tori asked.

"I don't... know. I don't think so. It was just... a really good kiss. But it was wrong in so many ways."

"If it was just a random kiss, then I'm sure you can get past it. Things like that happen, and if you're both mature, then it doesn't have to mean anything." Carla was speaking slowly, obviously thinking through the issue as she did. "But if you both want your relationship to change, then why shouldn't it?"

"I just said. I'm not sure... I do. And I don't think Jace..." She trailed off, trying to fight a tiny swell of excitement at the idea that Jace might actually be interested in something more than friendship from her.

She'd never even considered it before. But maybe... maybe...

"Has Jace ever said anything about changing your relationship?" Tori asked, her voice strangely gentle.

"No," Isabella admitted.

"Has he ever made any moves? Any romantic gestures? Anything?"

Isabella shook her head, feeling that little swell of excitement shrink at this knowledge.

"Was he the one who kissed you this morning?"

"No. It was... it was my idea."

She hated to admit it because it placed the blame for the situation entirely on her. But it was her fault. She was the one who'd gotten them into the situation. She had no idea what she'd been thinking—or if she'd been thinking at all.

If only she could go back in time and take back the morning—make it never have happened.

The world wouldn't allow do-overs though, so she was stuck with her own stupidity.

Tori had been silent for a moment, but now she asked, "Do you have any reason to think he's interested in more than friendship?"

Isabella sighed and shook her head mutely.

"Then he isn't. After all these years, if he was interested in you, he would have told you."

"Unless he's afraid..." Isabella trailed off, knowing even as she began that the sentiment was foolish.

"If guys are really interested, they let you know. It's only girls who read all kinds of romantic stuff and deep meaning into their nonexistent actions. You know that."

Isabella nodded. One result of having three sisters was having plenty of experience in watching guys interact with girls. "I know. But he did... he did seem to enjoy the kiss."

"Of course he did. He's a guy. If you give a guy the chance to kiss you, almost all of them will take you up on it. It doesn't mean that he wants more—unless he both tells you and shows you he wants more."

Carla had been letting Tori do most of the talking, but now she interjected, "If he hasn't told you and showed you he wants a relationship, then odds are he doesn't. Don't get hung up on one kiss. If you start hoping for something to happen between you without a clear signal from him, then that's really going to mess up your friendship."

"I won't." Isabella squared her shoulders. The little fluttering excitement inside her was completely dead now, but she felt more like herself. She wasn't going to be stupid. Not anymore. "I'm sure it was nothing. Jace has never done anything—not *anything*—to make me think he wants to be more than my friend."

"Then he doesn't." Tori seemed pleased with her sister's common-sense approach, and she reached into her bag to pull out a slightly crumpled piece of paper. "Here. I was saving this for you, and this seems like a good time."

Isabella took the paper and read the title in large font. *Speed Dating*.

"It's one of those speed dating things. Next weekend. There's still time for you to sign up. I thought it might be a good way for you to meet a lot of guys at once instead of wasting so many evenings on loser dates."

Isabella scanned the information and tried to summon some sort of excitement.

The truth was, she wanted to go home and daydream about kissing Jace again.

But that was wrong. And that was foolish. And that was only asking for heartache.

Plus, more importantly, that would seriously get in the way of a friendship that was one of the most important things in her life.

She wasn't going to mess things up. She was smarter than that.

"That's not a bad idea," she said.

"It's perfect. Maybe you'll meet your Prince Charming there and forget all about that kiss with Jace."

Maybe. But Isabella wasn't sure that would happen any time soon.

She stayed at her parents' house until early afternoon, when she had to go to work in the beauty salon. She was always busy on Saturday afternoons, so she didn't have much time to dwell on Jace and what had possessed her to kiss him that morning.

He called once at about three, but she didn't take calls when she was working, so she figured it wasn't wrong to just ignore his call for the time being.

She had no idea what to say to him.

She was leaving the salon and heading to her apartment down the block when she stopped suddenly.

Jace was standing directly in front of her.

"Oh," she said, swallowing hard. "Hi."

"Hi." He was watching her soberly, not even a hint of a smile on his agile mouth.

"I've been working," she explained, gesturing toward the salon.

"I know. That's why I'm waiting here, so I can catch you as you leave."

"I saw you called. I just didn't have time…" She trailed off. There was no sense in lying to him. He knew she wanted to avoid him.

He knew her better than anyone else.

"Can we talk?" he asked, his eyes searching her face, as if looking for signs of whatever she was feeling.

What if he was afraid she was interested in him now?

What if he wanted to break it to her easy?

She cleared her throat and nodded. "We can walk down to the river if you want."

The downtown of Preston was made up of two blocks of cute, renovated shops and restaurants plus a half-mile walk by the river with benches and a couple of landmark signs. They walked in silence until they found a bench, where they sat down.

"I'm sorry I ran away this morning," Isabella burst out, wanting to get the conversation over with. "I was just embarrassed and confused and... and I ran."

"I understand."

"But I don't want anything to mess up our friendship. It was just a... a fluke or something."

"Is that what you think?" He was searching her expression again, and she had no idea what he was looking for.

Hopefully not signs of a broken heart or something. "I don't know exactly what it was, but we can just move on from it, can't we? I mean we've been friends for too long for something like this to come between us. You don't want that, do you?"

"I don't want anything to come between us, no," he said slowly.

She released a gust of relief. "So we'll be okay then. I mean my feelings haven't changed at all for you. Yours haven't changed, have they?"

He stared at her for a long time—almost frozen—before said softly, "My feelings haven't changed."

"So the kiss was just a fluke. Please say we can just forget it ever happened. Please, Jace." She reached out to grab his arm. "I'd completely fall apart if our friendship ever changed."

His lips parted, and he let out a strange little breath. "Okay. Let's forget it ever happened."

She smiled and reached out to hug him. It took a moment, but he finally hugged her back.

As she pulled away, she was more conscious than normal of his warm, hard body, of the physicality in his fingers, his jaw, in the shape of his shoulders.

She suddenly imagined kissing him again.

It took a moment, but she managed to shake those stray thoughts away. They were just the result of the kiss that morning, but they wouldn't linger forever.

She'd known and loved Jace for years without kissing or sex or bodies getting in the way of their relationship. It might take a few days, but she'd get back there eventually.

She had to.

Clearing her throat, she pulled out the flyer Tori had given her about the speed dating event. "Look," she said. "I'm going to go to this thing next weekend. You should sign up for it too. It would be fun for us to go together."

He frowned as he read the writing on the paper. "I don't know."

"Come on, Jace. Do it for me. I bet you'd have fun, and maybe you'd meet someone. We could double-date!" She sounded more excited about that prospect than she felt, but it was absolutely essential that they move on from that morning.

It was the only way out of this mess she'd landed them in.

He sighed and glanced away from her. For a moment, he almost looked defeated.

Then he turned back with a little smile. "Sure. I'll go. Why not?"

8

Worst. Idea. Ever.

Seriously, what was he thinking in agreeing to this? And worse than that, why the hell hadn't he tried to convince Isabella that this was a bad idea for her as well?

"Wow! Look at how many people are here," she said as she stood beside him, scanning the trendy, generic bar—one of the most recent additions to minimal nightlife in Preston. It was wall-to-wall people. Jace had no idea there were this many single people living in the area. "Is it weird that none of these people look familiar?"

He shook his head. "I guess people were willing to drive from all the surrounding towns for this. I had no idea this was actually a thing."

"Me either." Isabella paused and looked around some more. "Should we mingle? Get a drink? Or maybe—"

Her words were cut off by the sound of a loud bell.

"Can I have everyone's attention? The number each of

you was given at the registration table is your starting point—meaning that is where you are supposed to go and sit for your first date. Each one will last for three minutes, and then I'll ring the bell, and the ladies will stay where they are, and the gentlemen will rise and move on to the next table. Everyone understand?"

Jace watched as the overenthusiastic female host held up numbers and a bell to demonstrate for those in the room that didn't grasp the concept of those items. (Clearly speed daters must be clueless based on this demonstration.) He was just about to say that to Isabella when their host spoke again.

"You have also all been given cards with your names on it to hand out to those you feel a connection to and wish to see again—you know, for a real date! And believe me, you'll probably find more than one. There's good energy in the room tonight. Don't you think so?" The host's smile was way too bright.

Jace had to refrain from rolling his eyes.

The woman was in her late forties to early fifties—if he was being generous—and wearing a leopard-print dress two sizes too small. She had big hair and loud makeup and was showing way too much cleavage.

Clearly this wasn't her first rodeo.

"Now I know some of you are shy and may feel a little uncomfortable with making small talk, but you should try to just stick to the basics. You only have three minutes, and you want to make sure that each of you has a chance to share something about yourself. Don't be an oversharer, but don't be too quiet!"

Seriously, was this thing for real? Unable to help himself, he leaned over and whispered in Isabella's ear, "This is a little like the Three Bear's scenario—don't talk to long, don't talk to short, talk just right."

Beside him, she giggled and swatted him playfully on the arm.

Maybe he stayed close a little longer than was necessary, but damn did she smell good. Really good. Good enough to taste.

Slowly.

All over.

From head to toe.

Leaning in a little bit more, he discreetly inhaled as his eyes slowly closed. God, what would it be like to have the freedom to do this and then take her by the hand and lead her back to his place? It may not be the perfect time, but if he could just...

The damn bell rang out again.

"Everyone to your tables please! We're ready to begin!"

"Oh! It's time! Exciting!" Isabella spoke with a familiar mocking enthusiasm—as if she were excited but making fun of it at the same time—but Jace sensed her mood was a little forced. Her smile didn't quite meet her eyes. Was it possible that she wasn't as thrilled to be here as she was leading him to believe?

"Bella, are you sure—"

"I am. This is gonna be good. Right? I mean, look at all the people here. Wouldn't it be great if we both met someone tonight? And then we could double-date and go out and—"

He placed his hands on her shoulders to stop her. "Bella, you're babbling. What's going on?"

"Nothing," she said quickly. "I... I guess I'm just a little nervous. I wasn't expecting quite so many people."

Jace looked around and sighed miserably. "Yeah. Me either."

Reaching up, Isabella squeezed one of his hands. She was about to say something, but the bell rang out—yet again—with the one-minute warning.

"Okay, we better get to our tables," Isabella said. She gave him a smile and a thumbs-up as she took a step back. "Good luck."

He didn't want luck. Not here. He wanted *her*, dammit! Why couldn't he just freaking admit it and get the hell out of here? "Bella, I—"

The noise in the room was too loud. She was swallowed up by the crowd as she made her way toward the back of the bar to her table. Jace looked down at his number and groaned. *Three.* So he was all the way in the front, and she was all the way in the back.

Great.

It would be at least an hour before they were at the same table.

Like a man going to his execution, he made his way to Table Three and had to stifle a groan.

Cougar.

The woman smiling up at him was easily in her fifties. She could have been the host's clone with her too-tight clothes and too-big hair. Ugh. If this was how the night was kicking off, he was already ready for it to end.

"Oh, my," the cougar purred. "Aren't you yummy!" She held out her hand to him. "I'm Tammy. And you are?"

Very sorry to be here, he almost said.

Not wanting to be rude—he was raised better than that—he shook her hand as he sat down. "Jace."

"Such a sexy name," she said, leaning forward to show him way too much cleavage.

The bell rang out.

"Okay, people! Let's speed date!"

There was a possibility that Jace had met some nice, eligible women over the course of the evening, but he couldn't say so with any great certainty. Mainly because he had been so distracted by trying to catch a glimpse of Isabella with each of her dates. Every time he moved a little bit closer, his anxiety grew. The closer he got, the more he could see her smiles or hear her laugh, and each time he had to ask himself if she was actually having a good time and making a connection with any of these guys.

He seriously hoped not.

"...so I teach tenth grade biology, and let me tell you, it's as brutal as it sounds."

Forcing himself to focus, Jace smiled at the blonde sitting across from him. She was cute, he guessed, but there was definitely no spark.

"I always enjoyed science classes," he said conversationally and then leaned to the right to see who Isabella was talking to.

The blonde turned around and then back again. "Is that your ex?"

"What?"

"The girl back there that you keep looking at. Is she an ex-girlfriend or something?"

Busted.

"No. No. She's just a friend."

She nodded sympathetically. "But you wish she was more." It wasn't a question.

Why try denying it. "Pretty much. I'm here to be supportive, and I thought it was a good idea, but now? Not so much."

"Wow. Sorry. Been there, done that. Does she know how you feel?"

He shook his head. "I'm afraid if she finds out, I'll lose the friendship. And I definitely don't want to do that."

"What if you don't lose the friendship? What if she feels the same way, and then you go on to have this great future together?"

If only it were that easy, he thought to himself.

"If it were going to happen, it would have by now," he said miserably. "Look, I'm sorry. You seem like a very nice woman, and it's not fair to you that I'm not here for the right reasons."

She waved him off. "Everyone's here for different reasons, and not everyone is looking for a serious date. I've gotten four offers for sex—no strings—and three offers to fix me up with their friends. So really, you being here to support a friend that you have feelings for? That's probably the sweetest thing I've heard all night."

"You're being far too kind," he said with a small smile. "I hope that you meet someone tonight who's good and decent and appreciates that about you."

She smiled at him. "Thanks, Jace."

The bell rang, and Jace moved on. Only two more "dates" to go before he was at Isabella's table. Doing his best, he put some effort into engaging with each one and even forced himself to not look in Isabella's direction. But as soon as the bell rang out to announce he could get to her, he nearly fell out of his chair to get there.

"Hey, there," he said with a smile and sat down on the bar stool. "I'm Jace. I'm a Sagittarius, I work for the town of Preston. I enjoy a good burger and watching old Monty Python movies."

Isabella laughed, her head falling back as she did. When she looked at him, her smile took his breath away. She decided to play along and introduced herself.

"It's nice to meet you, Jace. I'm Isabella. I'm a hair stylist who dabbles in cosmetology. I work for a salon here in Preston. I also enjoy a good burger, but I'm a sucker for a romantic comedy."

He sighed dramatically. "Well, I guess we gave it a try. Good luck to you!"

She laughed again and then reached out and grabbed both his hands in hers. "Oh, I'm so glad you're finally here. This has been the worst!" she said in a hushed tone. "There are a lot of creepy guys out there."

"That's what I've been hearing."

Releasing his hands, she sat back in her seat a bit and sighed. "And we've still got another half hour to go."

"We could leave right now. Go grab a burger—or ice cream," he said with a wink, knowing it was one of her weaknesses, "and pick a movie on Netflix and call it a night."

She grabbed one of his hands again and squeezed. "Seriously, this is the best date I've had all night, Jace. And as tempting as the ice cream and movie sounds, I need to stick this out. For all I know, my dream guy is going to be in this next batch—maybe even the last guy I talk to."

It was on the tip of his tongue to tell her it was highly unlikely, but he kept it to himself. "How about afterward? When all this is over, we'll grab something to eat and compare notes."

She smiled. "That sounds perfect. Thanks."

The bell rang out, and he was forced to move on— disappointed that his last round of dates would have him sitting with his back to her as he made his way around the other side of the bar.

Jace waited by the door for Isabella. Throngs of people walked by on their way out—most of them smiling and laughing. When he caught a glimpse of Isabella, however, she wasn't.

"What's wrong?" he asked. "Are you okay?"

"I just want to leave," she murmured. "Can we just go?"

Nodding, he placed a hand on the small of her back and guided her out the door. "Bella, what's wrong? What happened? Did someone upset you?"

She said nothing as they made their way to his car. Then she spun around and faced him. "What is *wrong* with me?" she cried out. "Can you please just tell me what it is?"

"Wrong? I don't understand."

A loud huff was her only response before she tried opening the car door. He hadn't unlocked it yet, and he quickly hit the remote to do so. Isabella climbed into the car and slammed the door, and Jace hung his head and opened his door and braced himself for whatever it was she had to say.

But she didn't say anything.

They made it all the way back to her place without uttering a single word.

It wasn't until they were parked in front of her building that she finally turned to him.

"I had thirty-two dates tonight. Thirty-two! And not one of them asked for my card." Tears welled up in her eyes. "I was propositioned by a couple of creeps, got offers to be fixed up with some of their friends or brothers—and even two sisters!—but no one wanted to date me, Jace. It was like none of those guys were even looking for a serious relationship!"

He sighed and pulled her into his embrace—not an easy task in the confines of the car and with the console between them. "I'm sorry. I really am. I know how much you wanted this to work."

She rested her head on his shoulder. "I really did." It didn't take long for him to feel her tears through his shirt.

Dammit. He hated when she cried.

"Bella, you can't take this personally. If it makes you feel any better, I got propositioned by some pretty forward women. Mostly ones that were almost as old as my mom."

She let out a quiet laugh and lifted her head. "Promise you're not just saying that to make me feel better?"

He chuckled softly, wiping away her tears. "And I was even offered a date with someone's uncle. So you see? It was creepiness all around."

Her shoulders sagged. "I just don't get it. We're good people, aren't we?"

He nodded.

"We're nice and fun and attractive?"

He nodded again.

"Then why can't we find normal people to date us?" she asked sadly.

He didn't think now was the time to mention the eight cards he had in his pocket. Truth be known, he just hadn't wanted to hurt anyone's feelings by declining their card. There was no way he was going to actually call any of them. The only date he wanted was sitting right here in front of him.

They sat in companionable silence for a few minutes before Isabella pulled back. "I have a small variety of ice cream inside. And Netflix. Would you... I mean I know we normally do that at your place, but would you like to come in and hang out for a while?"

"Bella..."

"Please, Jace. I just... this night just really messed with me, and I need some time with my best friend. Please."

Shit. There was no way he could deny her anything.

With a sympathetic smile, he turned off the car and hoped that he'd be able to handle being alone with her and not do anything stupid.

Like say "I told you so" about this whole speed dating idea.

9

ISABELLA HAD WANTED JACE TO COME IN AND SPEND THE evening with her, but as soon as he walked in, she started feeling confused and self-conscious.

He was *there*—right there in her hallway. Tall and solid and adorably rumpled with the sexiest, slightly heavy-lidded eyes she'd ever seen.

Her best friend. Who was somehow morphing into something more in her muddled mind.

She gulped and turned to hurry into the kitchen.

As she was standing in front of the refrigerator, she couldn't remember what she'd been coming in here to get in the first place. Seeing a bottle of red wine she'd bought the other day, she grabbed it from the counter and started to open it, pleased to have something to do with her hands.

She poured a glass and offered it to Jace.

He took it with a little smile, his eyes studying her face

with the slightest hint of confusion. "I thought we were going to have ice cream."

Shit. Ice scream. That was what she had come in here to get.

"I... I decided I wasn't very hungry. But you can have ice cream if want."

He shook his head and shook his head. "Nah. This is fine. Thanks." After a pause, he added, "You okay?"

"Of course," she replied, forcing a smile. After she poured herself a glass of wine, she leaned against the counter, trying to act natural and casual when she felt anything but.

She'd been feeling incredibly needy, incredibly close to Jace. And she'd wanted nothing more than to spend the evening cuddled up beside him. But now that he was actually in her house, she realized she wanted even more than that.

She wanted to kiss him again.

She wanted to touch him all over.

She wanted him to touch her.

Her mind kept screaming about how wrong this was, but she couldn't seem to help her.

She desperately needed something to distract her. "So what do you want to do?"

Jace blinked. "I thought... Netflix?"

Damn! She couldn't even keep track of what she'd said five minutes ago.

Desperately searching for an alternative she might

reasonably suggest to make up for her gaffe, she stalled. "I know. I did say that. But... I don't know. I kind of want..."

Jace took a step closer to her, something shifting in his expression that made her breath hitch. "You want what, Bella?"

She gulped. "I want..." In a panic, she thought of a somewhat reasonable explanation for her behavior, and she took it. "Remember when we were in high school, and I was depressed or fighting with Brock, we would stay up late playing Scrabble?"

Jace smiled, although something inside him seemed to slump behind the expression, so subtle she never would have noticed if she hadn't known him so well. "Of course I remember." He took a slightly ragged breath. "You want to play Scrabble?"

It was a relief—a deep relief—to break the strange tension of the moment before. Plus the game might distract her from all these inappropriate thoughts and feelings she was having. "Is that all right?"

Jace took a big sip of wine. "Sure. Why not?"

An hour later, they'd almost finished the bottle of wine, and Isabella had to take a break to go to the bathroom and splash some water on her face.

She was feeling better—warm and amused and affectionate, not as scared as she'd been when they'd first arrived—but she was still finding Jace far too attractive, despite the familiarity of the game.

Blowing out a rush of air, she told herself to focus. *Focus.*

Scrabble was what was important at the moment. Nothing else.

"I'm telling you," Isabella called as she left the bathroom and headed back to the living room. "It's not a word."

"It is a word." Jace grabbed his phone and pulled up the dictionary app he used. "It has something to do with oxygen. You'll see."

"It's a prefix," she said, reminding herself he wasn't nearly as hot as he appeared to her at the moment. It was just the mixture of alcohol and neediness. That was all it was. "But it doesn't stand as a word on its own."

She'd changed clothes a little while ago so she could be comfortable as they played. She was now dressed in a stretchy T-shirt and plaid cotton pants that strongly resembled pajama bottoms. Jace knew better than to call them pajama pants, of course. He'd learned that the hard way a long time ago. They were "lounge pants."

When Jace found the appropriate entry, his face reflected a surge of relief that made it clear he hadn't been entirely confident in his grammatical claim. "Oxy," he read out loud, "Containing oxygen."

"But it's a prefix! If it says it's a prefix, then it doesn't count as a whole word, and you can't use it."

Jace smiled down at her as he showed her his phone.

"It says it can be a prefix, yes. But look. It can also be used adjectively."

Leave it to him to be able to use the word "adjectively" even after having downed three glasses of wine.

Isabella wasn't feeling as competitive as she really should be feeling. In fact, she was having trouble not smiling sappily at his adorably pompous expression. "Fine. Whatever."

Jace chuckled as she took her place on the floor across from him.

The Scrabble game continued, and Isabella eventually started growing suspicious as Jace clearly began preserving certain of his letters. She knew what that expression and strategy of his meant.

He had a great word, and he was just waiting for the opportunity to use it.

She was more suspicious than ever when he put down a T and E around an H to form the word "the." He never would have put down such a waste of a turn if he wasn't waiting for something phenomenal.

They were tied at the moment, but she had a little feeling they wouldn't be for long.

"Uh-oh," she said, trying to sound like she would have sounded on any other evening with Jace. "That's your snotty face. You must think you have a good move."

Jace frowned too, clearly not appreciating being called "snotty." But he ignored it, obviously more interested in his word.

She'd put down the word "roast" a few moves ago, and she watched as he started laying down tiles around it.

When he put down the Z tile on the Triple Word Score Square, Isabella made a little squeak. When he added R-I-A-N at the end of the word "roast," thus including yet another Triple Word Score Square, she made a choking sound.

Looking quite proud of himself, Jace admired his completed word. Giving her a look of exaggerated mildness, he murmured, "I believe that should be 180 points."

"Zoroastrian?" she read aloud, sitting upright as she stared at him.

He nodded. "Zoroastrian."

"But... but..." She was sputtering, her slightly clouded mind trying to catch up to this indignation. "But that's a proper noun!"

He shook his head. "Nonsense."

"Yes, it is! It's that old religion, isn't it?"

Jace's face was perfectly composed, but she could tell he was greatly enjoying both his word and this argument. "Yes, originally the word was used to identify a follower of Zoroastrianism. But now the word has moved beyond that specific context, so it's no longer a proper noun."

Isabella's mouth dropped open, hardly believing his nerve in suggesting such a thing.

"It has, Isabella. That's the way language works."

"But it would still always be capitalized! That's against the rules!" She was shifting between glaring at the word on the board and glaring at Jace's guileless face.

"No, it wouldn't. Not when it's used as a generic adjective."

"Use it noncapitalized in a sentence."

"She had a traditional, Zoroastrian perspective on life, although she liked to consider herself a nouveau thinker."

He was bluffing. He had to be. But he was doing it well —straight-faced and steady eyed, with both his hands and his mouth relaxed.

Isabella's outrage flickered a little as she suddenly wondered if he was right.

He'd always been so smart. It was one of the things she loved about him.

"You had that ridiculous sentence planned all this time," she said.

"Maybe. But it doesn't mean I'm not right."

She stared at him fixedly until she saw the corner of his mouth twitch just slightly.

"I knew it! You're bluffing!"

"Never." He was obviously still trying to hold on to his composure, but his eyes were brimming with humor, and he was having trouble hiding a smile.

"Cheater!" Bursting into laughter, she tackled him, playfully pushing him down so he was lying on his back on the floor. "You're cheating, and you know it, so you have to forfeit the game."

She realized her mistake when Jace's hard, lean body started to rub against hers. Her heart began to race with excitement as her breath quickened and shivers of excitement ran up and down her spine.

His hand slowly slid down her back until he was cupping her hips, almost—almost—touching her bottom. "I'll never forfeit. I'll go to my death declaring that Zoroastrian is a perfectly legitimate Scrabble word."

Despite his light tone, his expression had changed again. His eyes were hot. So hot. As hot as she felt.

She couldn't stop herself from rubbing against him again, and she suddenly realized how tense his body was.

Tense. And tight. And hard.

So hard.

All of him hard.

He shifted beneath her weight, and every little move he made against her fired all her sensitized nerve endings.

She wanted him to roll over on top of her. Sink into her completely.

She wanted him to bury himself in her and never come out.

Jace closed his eyes and took a slightly shaky breath, and she knew now why that was.

He was aroused beneath her. She could feel it very starkly when she rubbed her pelvis against his.

She made a breathless noise at the realization, and she trailed her hand down his chest to his belly.

Jace jerked in what looked like surprised pleasure.

"Jace?" she whispered, her hand grazing down even farther.

It felt like there was some sort of magnetic force drawing her hand down toward the bulge of his erection.

He was sweating a little—she could see it—and his breath was blowing in and out in short huffs.

He grunted, not really forming a complete word.

Isabella's hand had reached his belt, and she idly played with the supple leather. Maybe it was the wine. Or maybe she'd been holding back for too long.

But she heard herself saying, "I know that we're just friends, and that we said that kiss didn't mean anything. I know touching like this is really against the rules."

Her hand slipped down even lower, brushing against the bulge at the front of his trousers. Jace let out a soft strangled sound in response, as if he were desperately trying to hold himself back.

The knowledge was all she needed to know.

He wanted this just as much as she did.

"But I was wondering," Isabella continued, lifting her upper body so she could look down on his strained face, "if maybe we could break that rule... a little."

Jace's back arched up slightly as she palmed his arousal. "Isabella," he rasped. "What..."

At any other moment, she never would have said this out loud, but there was no way to stop herself now. "I want you, Jace. Please. Don't make me wait anymore."

He groaned helplessly, clearly giving up on his resistance. He took hold of her and rolled them over so he was on top of her. Then he kissed her fiercely.

She clutched at his hair and rocked into him as their tongues tangled and dueled. Nothing had ever felt so good, so right.

Nothing was as good as this.

She was so aroused now she couldn't lie still. She kept trying to grind herself against him, trying to ease the pulsing ache between her legs.

Repositioning himself again so he could make better use of his hands, he cupped one of her breasts over her shirt, brushing the hard nipple with his thumb. "Can I...," he began, his voice so thick she barely recognized it.

"Yeah." She arched her back, lifting her breasts into his touch, and her eyes fell shut as he caressed her. "God, yeah."

Her blood, her pulse, her heart were all throbbing with her body as he moved in nearly slow motion, stroking her breasts, her belly, and then lower.

"Yes," she gasped, lifting her hips as his agile fingers moved beneath her waistband.

He teased her for a few minutes until he slid a finger inside her. He couldn't possibly mistake how wet and aroused she already was, and he added a second finger and started to pump them slowly, watching her face as if he trying to learn her responses.

She sucked in an urgent breath and tried to grind her pelvis against his hand, her hands clutching at the rug beneath her.

With this encouragement, Jace lowered his head until he could mouth one of her breasts through her shirt. He sucked and twirled her nipple with his tongue, until the thin fabric was so damp it was transparent and Isabella was mewling with pleasure.

He started curling up his fingers as he pumped them inside her, a shift that caused Isabella to buck her hips up against his hand and pant out a lot of loud, breathless sounds.

His mouth still working on her breast, he murmured, "Isabella? Can you come?"

His question made her halt her shameless squirming and give him a half-dazed look. "Um, I'm not quite there yet."

He huffed with amusement. "I meant," he explained, still nuzzling against her nipple, "is this working for you? You'll have to tell me what you like."

She giggled warmly and moved one of her hands to the back of his head, stroking his hair. "I like this. It's definitely working."

He shifted his hand so that his thumb could rub against her clit, and her amusement vanished as she cried out sharply and her back bent up in an involuntary arc.

"God!" Isabella gasped, tossing her head and squeezing her eyes shut. Nothing in the world had ever felt like this— like Jace, her Jace, touching her this way, making her feel so good. "Oh, God!"

Then all the excruciating tension shattered as she came, her muscles clenching hard around his fingers and her body convulsing as she cried out her pleasure.

He watched her as she came. She knew he did, and it made everything even hotter.

Before she'd even caught her breath, he was kissing her again. She couldn't seem to keep her hands off him now.

She pulled eagerly at his clothes, wanting to touch his skin, wanting to see his body in a way she never had before.

They couldn't seem to stop kissing, even as they fumbled with their clothes, even as they were both naked, their skin touching intimately at last.

And they still couldn't stop kissing, even as he was settling between her legs and she was trying to guide him inside her body.

"Wait," he grunted. "Condom."

She sucked in a ragged breath, trying to clear her mind enough to think through whether she even had one in the house.

"In my pocket," Jace said, as if he'd just remembered himself.

Since he was so tense he was shaking with it, she managed to sit up and search his clothes until she found the condom. Then he was on top of her again, kissing her, stroking her, rolling on the condom, and finally—finally—moving inside her.

She cried out at the tight penetration, and she could see his features twist as if he were just as affected as she was.

It was so right. So exactly right. Having him inside her this way.

No one had ever been closer to her than Jace. And no one ever would be. And this felt like the culmination of that truth.

At last.

After a minute, he seemed to get control of himself, and he started to move. She could tell he was trying to keep his thrusts slow and steady, but he was failing utterly. He couldn't hold back, and she didn't want him to.

She bent her knees up around his hips and rocked with him, clawing at his back and urging him on with loud pants and little squeezes. Her body was tightening again. It knew what it wanted.

And knew that Jace was the one who could give it.

"Jace," she gasped as all the pleasure rose up in a wave. He was taking her hard and fast now, exactly as she needed. "Jace!"

"Yes, Bella. Yes, baby." His grunts were low and hoarse and almost helpless. She'd never before seen him like this. "I want you to come, baby."

She cried out as the tension released inside her, her body shuddering in the wake of intense feelings. She was saying his name over and over again as he grunted a few more times and came too, hard, uninhibited, completely.

Then they collapsed together, holding on to each other.

Isabella had never known it was possible to feel so completely sated, like there was nothing else in the world she could possibly want.

Just Jace. Like this.

Eventually, however, she started to get a little cold, and he started to feel a bit heavy on top of her.

When she shifted, he pulled off, rising to his knees to shake himself off and then take care of the condom.

Being naked just a minute before had felt perfectly natural, but now she was hit with a sudden wave of self-consciousness.

What had just happened? What was Jace thinking now? What if everything between them would change and never go back to what they'd had before?

She reached for her clothes and pulled them back on. The skin on her bottom and shoulder blades were rubbed slightly raw from having sex on the floor like this.

She hadn't even realized it while it was happening.

"Are you okay?" he asked quietly, zipping up his pants and reaching for his shirt.

"Yeah." When her voice broke, she cleared her throat and tried again. "Yes. The rug's not actually the most comfortable place to have sex."

"I guess not."

His voice was so soft, so careful, that she finally had to look him in the eye to see what he was thinking.

Even looking at his face, she couldn't tell.

"Jace," she began, her mouth twisting with a sudden surge of panic.

"Let's not do that," he interrupted, before she could get anything said.

"Do what?"

"Overanalyze everything. We both wanted this. It was good. Really good. And we're still friends. We'll always be friends. Right?"

She nodded, relieved by the confidence in his words.

That was what mattered the most, after all. "But what... I mean how are we going to..."

"Let's just play it by ear. If something happens, it happens. I don't think trying to figure everything out right now, on the floor, after a bottle of wine and the best sex of my life, is really going to lead to any deep understandings."

She sucked in a breath that caught just slightly. Intense relief was washing over her. Maybe they didn't have to hash everything out right now.

It was sex. Great sex.

He'd said it was the best sex of his life.

It was definitely the best of hers.

But they were still friends. They'd always be friends. And they could just see what happened from here on out.

They didn't have to figure everything out about their relationship right now.

He was watching her closely, and he seemed to see her relief. It evidently relieved him too. He smiled fondly. "All right?" he asked. "Does that sound okay?"

"It sounds... great." She dropped her eyes, feeling suddenly shy. "But... I mean... will we do this again?"

"If we want to. That's what it means to just see what happens."

She nodded, relieved by this too—because the truth was she definitely wanted this to happen again. "So nothing really changes. We just have sex again if we want to?"

"Right. We just let things happen as they happen."

There was something about his posture and expression

that made her think he was being careful—very careful, like he was afraid the wrong word would send a tower of cards toppling over.

She could understand that. This was the kind of thing that could destroy a friendship.

But they didn't have to let that happen.

She wasn't sure how she could survive if that happened.

"Okay," she said at last. "Good. So what do we do now?"

"What do you want to do?"

"I... I think I need some water."

He smiled. "All right then. You do that, and I'll clean up the Scrabble board."

Her heart skipped a beat in a ridiculous way.

"It's really too bad," he said in a different tone. His normal teasing one. "I was on the cusp of a remarkable victory."

Isabella snorted. "You were on the cusp of being a big cheater. Zoroastrian. Right."

"You're just jealous because you weren't the author of such a piece of brilliance."

"I'm not a Scrabble cheater." She managed to stand up, slightly sore between the legs in a way that made her feel ridiculously fluttery. And a little proud. Then she remembered she was supposed to go get some water.

She was walking toward the kitchen when she was hit by a surge of fear and turned back to look at Jace.

He'd been pushing a hand through his messy hair with

the strangest expression on his face. She couldn't even begin to interpret what it might mean.

When he saw her looking back at him, his face cleared, and he smiled again.

"You're sure it's going to be okay?" she asked.

"Of course it will. We love each other, right?"

She nodded. "Yes."

"Then we'll make sure it's fine."

She felt better at the words, at the reassurance. "Okay. Thanks."

"Of course." Then his eyes took on that warm, teasing look again and he added in a lazy drawl, "When you think about it, it's all very Zoroastrian."

10

"I LOATHE MYSELF," JACE MUTTERED AS HE KICKED HIS apartment door shut. The entire drive home from Isabella's had been spent calling himself every kind of idiot. "You had it. You had it all, and you just couldn't man the hell up and tell her how you felt. *Idiot.*"

"Idiot!" The voice echoed from across the room, and Jace groaned. Great. Now he'd have to deal with being mocked by the damn bird. Why hadn't he covered the cage when he'd left?

Stalking across the room, he was tempted to do just that, but decided that being mean to animals wasn't another bad move he was going to add to his resume. Beau had been in his cage all day, and Jace figured he might want to get out and fly around a bit. Opening the cage, he stepped back and waited. The bird blinked at him several times, and just when he was sure he wasn't going to fly out,

Beau fluttered and made his way out of the cage, squawking, "Idiot!"

"Awesome," Jace mumbled. "This is my life."

While Beau did his thing and stretched his wings, Jace changed into a pair of sweats and a T-shirt before grabbing a bottle of water and collapsing on the couch. It didn't matter how hard he tried, he couldn't seem to clear his mind of anything except how Isabella had felt as he'd sunk inside her.

God.

Never in his life had anything felt like that.

And how had he gone about letting her know? By saying they should *play it by ear.* He shook his head in disgust, just like he'd been doing for the past twenty minutes. So now what? How were they realistically supposed to move forward?

Sure, they could go back to the way things were and just chalk this up as a one-time thing. But he had a feeling Isabella wouldn't mind them doing it again. He knew he sure as hell wouldn't mind. If it were up to him, he'd be there right now, going for round two. Only this time they'd be in her bed, and he wouldn't be rushing.

Great. Now there was *that* image in his mind.

"Such a damn idiot," he muttered, taking a drink of water.

"Idiot!" Beau repeated.

So not what he needed right now—a snarky bird hammering the point home. He was about to get up and put Beau back in his cage when his phone dinged with an incoming text. Pulling it from his pocket, he looked down and smiled.

Isabella.

Thanks for going with me tonight her text read, and Jace had to let that sink in for a moment. It was such a benign comment—something that under normal circumstances wouldn't mean anything beyond the surface. But after what they'd done? He had to think about it. It didn't take long for him to realize that she was simply reaching out and looking for reassurance again that they were going to be all right.

What are friends for, right?

As soon as he hit send, he groaned. Could he seriously be any worse at this?

I'm so lucky to have you. That we have each other. I don't know what I'd ever do without you.

Jace stared at the phone for a few minutes. Should he call her? Stop this mild avoidance? His heart began to hammer in his chest, and he took a steadying breath.

You'll never have to find out. We'll always be friends.

Coward.

She instantly replied with a smiley face emoji and wished him a good night. He wished her one as well and threw his head back on the sofa cushion and blew out a breath. Beau landed beside him, tilted his head, and studied him.

Yeah, this pretty much summed up his life—he could

be in bed with Isabella right now, living out his every fantasy, but instead he was sitting on his couch with a bird.

"Idiot," Beau said.

And Jace didn't have it in him to argue.

A week later, Jace was still mildly confused.

But sexually satisfied.

With their promise to take things as they came and not let that one night change them, they stuck to their usual routine of seeing each other on an almost daily basis. The day after had been the most awkward. They had run into each other while grocery shopping and, at the sight of him, Isabella had instantly blushed.

And he had gotten instantly hard.

They ended up shopping together and laughing and joking as they always had, and by the time they'd checked out, Jace was convinced that he had imagined the hot sex of the previous night.

But then Isabella had shown up at his place that night out of the blue and... hell, he was still shocked by that one. He had opened the door and seen the hesitant look on her face, and he'd known. He'd known exactly what she was thinking because he was thinking it too. They made it as far as the couch.

Beau definitely learned some new words that night.

Harder.

Faster.

Yeah. The bird needed to go—especially if this relationship with Isabella kept going the way that it was. Nothing killed the moment faster than a bird mocking you at the height of passion.

Isabella hadn't said anything about it though. She didn't spend the night. If anything, she'd seemed just as shy and hesitant as she'd been when she arrived and then made an excuse about having to go home.

And like an idiot he hadn't stopped her.

Probably because he was still trying to catch his breath.

Yeah. She had come and gone that fast.

They'd texted on Sunday, but Jace was working on some reports for work and had been too bogged down with them to do anything but that. They'd gone to lunch Monday and Tuesday, and then he had been the one to pounce Tuesday night. Just the thought of it had him grinning. They had played a game of dirty Scrabble—not that it had started out that way—but sometimes when you had the right letters, you just had to play them.

Spank.

Deep.

Wet.

Horny.

Yeah, it didn't take a rocket scientist to figure out where his mind was, and Isabella had been completely on board. He reached behind him and blindly rubbed at a spot on his back where he was pretty sure there was still a letter X tile imprinted there.

They had kept their sexy shenanigans to themselves

and went about business as usual around town, so Jace wasn't sure why he was so surprised that people were still hell-bent on setting her up on dates.

But they were.

When he'd shown up at the salon on Wednesday, it hit him like a ton of bricks. Everyone was talking about the "great guy" they'd found for her and how they were certain he was "the one." Isabella had looked at him warily, and it was all Jace could do to keep a smile on his face and pretend that he didn't feel like he'd been kicked in the gut.

He was on the verge of telling her that he'd meet up with her later simply because he couldn't stand to hear any more details when she'd let out a scream and plastered herself against him.

With a sigh, his arm went around her. "Spider?"

She nodded and then looked over her shoulder. "Over there. By the wheel of my cart."

"You know it's probably more scared of you then you are of it, right?"

At this point, she would normally be pulling away.

But this time she wasn't. If anything, she pressed a little bit closer, and for a moment it was like they were alone in the room.

He wanted to comfort her as much as he wanted to tease her—and promise that he'd always be there to take care of her. His hand began to inch up to caress her cheek when...

"For crying out loud, Jace! Bend down and kill the

damn spider!" Mrs. Parker—his old seventh grade teacher —called out. "Then we can all admire how nice your butt looks in those jeans!"

All around them the ladies of the salon began to chime in on how cute his ass was, and all Jace wanted to do was crawl in a hole and die of embarrassment.

He chanced a look at Isabella, who was doing her best to not laugh along with the ladies, but a giggle came out, and then she stepped out of his embrace and laughed uninhibitedly. Of course, she still had the good sense to point to the spider. So without giving the lecherous hair brigade a show, he walked over and stomped on the spider and then grabbed a broom and took care of the carnage.

The collective sound of disappointment was rather good for his ego.

By the time they'd left and gone to grab something to eat, it was obvious that they had to deal with the elephant in the room.

"So you have a date Friday night," he said after they'd ordered their food.

Isabella nodded and took a long drink of her water.

"Is he anyone we know? Local?"

"Uh, no. He lives near Richmond but comes to Preston a lot on business."

"What does he do?"

She looked around and wouldn't quite meet his eyes. "He's a, uh, he's a doctor. He works with several clinics, volunteering his time. That sort of thing." She shrugged.

All he could do was nod. How the hell was he supposed to compete with a doctor? Wasn't that every girl's dream?

They sat in awkward silence for several minutes when Isabella finally let out a loud sigh and looked at him. "I didn't go out looking for this date, you know. But everyone is still trying to set me up, and since we're keeping *us* a secret, they wouldn't let me say no. I wasn't sure what else to do."

"It's fine."

She shook her head. "No, it's not. I knew this would happen. I knew things were going to get awkward. I can tell that you're not okay with me going out on this date."

Hell no, he wasn't. "Are *you* okay with going out on this date?" he countered, mainly to buy himself some time.

"What am I supposed to be?" she asked, her eyes wide. "We said we'd play this thing between us by ear, which is totally fine, but I can't just stop my life in the meantime. Tori's wedding will be here before we know it, and I'm no closer to finding... finding..." She trailed off, her eyes dropping and her shoulders slumping.

Finding the man of her dreams.

That was who she was looking for.

And no matter what had happened between them, evidently she hadn't found him yet.

"You want a man you can fall in love with," he said softly.

She nodded, looking back up to meet his eyes. "I do,

Jace. I really do. I mean, the sex is... is amazing, but love is more important to me than sex."

He let out a sigh, feeling like his heart had been ripped out of his chest. "Of course it is. So you want to... to go back to the way we were before?"

Her face twisted. "I don't know. Jace, I just don't know."

He suddenly saw that she was about to say something appalling, something about how maybe even their friendship had been changed because of the sex and they could never go back.

And he couldn't stand that—he couldn't let that happen.

"Well, we don't have to figure it out right now," he said quickly, speaking with a feigned casualness so she wouldn't see how urgent he was. "We said we'd just play things by ear, so that's what we'll do. You go out on your date, and we'll figure out everything else between us later on. Don't worry about it."

She nodded, looking relieved, but he could still see the worry in her eyes.

"Look, I want you to have everything you dream of, no matter what it is. If you think this guy has potential, then you should go out with him." It might have been the hardest sentence he'd ever spoken. "Although from the past few dates you've had, you might want an out."

"An out?"

"Yeah, you know, someone there to meet him with you and sort of give the thumbs-up or thumbs-down if things don't seem right."

"Oh. I hadn't thought of that." She paused and took another sip of her drink. "Would you do it? He's picking me up at my place and—"

"At your place? I thought you'd been meeting these guys at the restaurant so they wouldn't know where you lived in case things went south."

"I know. I was, but Cliff's a good guy, and everyone in town knows him, so I didn't think it was a big deal."

"Cliff? His name is Cliff? As in Clifford?"

Isabella made a face at him. "What's wrong with that?"

"You mean other than his name is the same as the big red dog?"

She rolled her eyes. "Stop it." But then she started to giggle. "Great, now that's all I'm going to be able to think of when I see him!"

Jace started laughing too, and for a few minutes they were relaxed. Happy. Just themselves.

"So you'll come to the house and meet him before the date?"

And they were back to awkward.

"Yeah. Sure. I'll be there."

Their meals arrived, and Jace was just about to take his first bite when Isabella's words stopped him.

"You really let the girls at the salon down by not bending over to kill the spider, you know."

He looked at her and saw her lips twitching. "Is that right?"

She nodded. "Definitely. You have quite a fan following in town."

This was news to him. "And you know this *how*?"

"Well, with all the talk of finding me a future husband, your name always comes up when sexy and good-looking guys are mentioned." They smiled at each other with a wry kind of amusement. "All I'm saying is that you should keep that in mind next time you're in the salon."

"What? Bending over and giving everyone a show? I'm not going to have to do a sexy dance or anything, am I?"

She giggled and gave him a mischievous grin. "Do you know how to do a sexy dance?"

"I guess you'll just have to wait and see."

They'd enjoyed the rest of their dinner, and he thought to himself, "This is it. The sex part of the relationship is over. She's not going to feel comfortable being with me that way again."

But when they'd walked out to their cars, Isabella hugged him... and bit his neck.

Then licked it.

Something inside him howled.

When she did it again, he hauled her close and growled her name. "Bella, don't..."

Then he shut up because, seriously, why was he fighting this? It was exactly what he wanted. He leaned in and did his own biting and licking until he felt her knees practically give out.

"My place," she'd panted as she rubbed up against him. "It's closer."

Who was he to argue?

On Friday night, he was back at her apartment, sitting on the sofa waiting for Cliff.

Clifford.

The doctor.

Not the dog.

The doorbell rang, and Isabella was still in her bedroom getting dressed. "Can you get that, Jace?"

"No problem," he called back. In his mind, he came up with a dozen scenarios where he could tell good ol' Dr. Cliff that he could take a hike, that Isabella wasn't interested.

But he didn't.

Partly because he was a decent guy.

And partly because the guy was built like a linebacker.

Not a good sign.

"Hey, I'm Cliff. I'm here for Isabella," the man said. He was easily over six feet tall, with jet black hair and gray eyes.

"I'm Jace. A... friend of Bella's. Come on in. She's still getting ready." They shook hands, and Jace led him into the living room. "Can I get you something to drink?" That seemed like the polite thing to do, didn't it?

Cliff looked at him hesitantly even as he looked around the room—as if searching for Isabella. "Uh, sure. Thanks."

"Beer?" Jace offered, hoping that if he said yes, it would be a strike against him for considering drinking and then driving.

"No, thanks. Water would be just fine."

Damn. "No problem. Make yourself comfortable." A minute later he was back with a bottle of water and sat himself in the oversized chair facing Cliff. "So Bella tells me you're a doctor."

Cliff nodded. "I am."

"Any specialties?"

"GP all the way. I travel to different hospitals and clinics and lend a hand wherever I'm needed."

"Don't like to stay in one place?" Jace asked, hoping to find that the guy would eventually take off and leave Isabella.

"I would love to, but I know how shorthanded so many of these places are, and I just want to be useful where I can."

Can't fault the guy for that either. Dammit. "But you just stay here in Virginia, right?"

"I did a couple of stints with Doctors Without Borders, but I missed my family too much. I'd go back if there was a real crisis situation, but my mom had a hip replacement, and my dad is struggling with complications from diabetes, so I'd rather be stateside if they need me."

Freaking Cliff was almost a saint.

Jace had to refrain from cursing.

"I'm sure they're happy to have you back home," he said miserably.

"And you're a friend of Isabella's?" Cliff asked, but it was sort of a rhetorical question. "I think it's nice that you're watching out for her. There are a lot of creeps out there. You're a good friend to be here to make sure she's okay."

Great. Now he was complimenting him too. Hell, at this rate, Jace might want to date him!

"Sorry to keep you waiting," Isabella said as she breezed into the room.

Jace was instantly assaulted by her sweet, floral scent and had to fight the urge to haul her over to him and demand that Cliff leave. She was dressed in a conservative-looking black dress, but still... damn. There was no way for her not to look sexy.

Cliff stood and greeted her, and Isabella looked cautiously between the two of them. Jace could only imagine how they looked—like day and night. They were so opposite. Part of him rationalized that there was no way she could possibly be attracted to a guy like Cliff when clearly she was attracted to him. But as he stood back and watched her smile at her date and how easily they fell into conversation with one another, he began to doubt himself.

And the relationship he thought was developing between him and Isabella.

Shit.

"Well, I guess we should get going," Isabella said, smiling. She grabbed a sweater that she'd had draped over the sofa and slipped it on. Turning to Jace she said, "I'll talk to you tomorrow, right?"

This would totally be the wrong time to say what was on his mind—to tell her that she had to choose right now between the two of them—but that didn't stop him from imagining how it would go. Unfortunately, he had a feeling Dr. Wonderful Humanitarian would win out in a big way, and then he'd be stuck standing here as a loser.

"Jace?" she prompted.

"Oh, yeah. Sure. Definitely."

"Where are you going tonight?" she asked as the three of them walked toward the door.

Home. He was going home to be alone. Well, not totally alone. There was Beau and all.

Maybe they'd take a bath together and complete his descent into being completely pathetic.

"I'm meeting some of the guys from work for poker," he lied.

"Oh, I love poker night!" she said with a bit of a pout and then seemed to catch herself. "I mean..."

Once in a while, she had joined him when he did get together with the guys to play. That wasn't why he'd mentioned it though. It was just the first thing to come to mind. "I'll tell everyone you said hello."

By now they were all out on the driveway, and Jace wished them a good night as he walked to his car. As he was opening the door, he stopped and watched as Cliff held the door for her and then walked around to get into his hybrid Lexus.

Because of course Cliff would be good to the environment too.

Dammit.

And as they pulled out of the driveway and drove away, Jace felt like his fate had been sealed.

They might remain friends, but he'd still lost Isabella for good.

11

A WEEK LATER, ISABELLA WOKE UP AT ABOUT TWO IN THE morning, hit with a surge of panic so overwhelming she gasped and sat up straight in the bed.

Jace's bed.

She'd fallen asleep with him earlier, after they'd had sex in slow, thorough silence.

Two weeks now, and they were still trying to maintain this precarious balance between sex and friendship. In daylight hours, she tried to talk herself into believing it was reasonable and understandable.

But deep inside she knew better.

Her skin was cold and clammy as she tried to catch her breath in the dark room. This was wrong. Something was deeply wrong with what they were doing.

They were endangering their friendship, and that was something she could never accept.

She'd been on the verge of breaking it off completely

when Jace had reacted so stiffly to news of her date with Cliff, but then he'd convinced her it wasn't a big deal after all.

But she knew inside that it was a big deal, no matter what Jace said.

She had to stop this. Now. Tonight would have to be the last night.

"Bella, baby? What's the matter?" Jace's voice was thick and sleepy—so incredibly sexy.

"Nothing." She tried desperately not to sound as breathless and shaky as she felt.

She obviously failed.

Jace sat up too. "Hey, don't lie to me. Tell me what's wrong."

With another ragged breath, she turned her head in his direction. It was too dark in the room to see him clearly, and somehow that made this conversation safer.

Jace had never lied to her. Not once in all the years she'd known him. She wasn't going to lie to him either.

"Are you sick?" he asked, reaching out until he could find and stroke her hair back from her face.

"No." Swallowing hard, she admitted, "I just... I just got scared. About what we're doing, I mean."

"Oh."

There was a strange timbre to his voice, and it made her stomach twist. Jace was incredible, but he was still a guy. And guys always got nervous and reluctant about conversations like this. What if he thought she'd decided she wanted more from him? What if he was already edging away from that possibility?

She would lose him. And she just couldn't lose him.

"It seems... I don't know. Something feels wrong about it. Like we're not being reasonable to expect to just keep doing what we're doing without ever really thinking it through."

Jace was silent for so long it terrified her. Then he said slowly, "I can understand that."

"I mean I'm just feeling... unsettled about it."

"Okay. So tell me what would make you feel more settled. What do you want?"

"I want..." She took a shaky breath and tried to clear her mind from the fog of fear and confusion. "I want to always be your friend."

"I've already told you that's never going to change. No matter what else happens, you're my best friend for the rest of my life."

Her eyes burned with a sudden swell of emotion at the hoarse sincerity in his tone. "Me too."

"Good. So what else do you want?"

It was easier with him questioning her like this. And it was easier in the dark. As if she could say things she'd be too self-conscious to admit in the light of day. "The sex is... is amazing. The best I've ever had."

"Me too."

"But I still want... I still want a man who will be the love of my life. A husband I can share life with, raise a family with. I've always wanted that, and I don't think it's going to change. No matter how good the sex is with you, it's never going to be enough."

There was a strange tension in his body. She could feel it, even though she couldn't see him. "So you... so you want more?"

"Yes." She frowned, not quite sure why he was asking such an obvious question. "Of course I want more. That's why I don't want to stop dating. But it feels wrong to have sex with you while I'm dating other guys. It feels... just wrong."

"It's not wrong." Jace's tone was different now, although she couldn't see his expression enough to know why. "I'm in this with both eyes open. If you're worried about me, then don't be."

She wasn't exactly worried about him in that way. She was worried about their friendship. But it didn't feel like she could say anything more. She wasn't even sure what she should say.

"I just... I just don't really know," she said at last.

She sat there, staring in his direction for a long time, until he finally said, "It's fine not to know. That's why we're just playing it by ear. There's nothing to worry about, Bella. And I can think of other things for us to be doing in bed together like this."

She recognized his shift in tone, and it was like a wave of relief washing over her. It was much more enjoyable to have sex with him than to try to figure out what was happening between them and what the consequences would be.

Maybe he was right.

Maybe they should just relax and take what was offered.

She lay back down with a long exhale and then giggled softly when he rolled over on top of her. "We were having a conversation," she said, smiling at him in the dark.

He rubbed himself against her, making it clear he was already getting hard. "Do you still want to talk?" he drawled. "Or do you want to do something else now?"

She pulled his head down so she could kiss him. "Definitely something else."

Three hours later, she was leaving Jace's apartment. It wasn't even six in the morning yet, and the building was utterly silent.

Which was why she gave a little jump when someone appeared from the door to the stairwell.

"Oh," Isabella said, catching her breath as she recognized the woman. "Mrs. Berry! Good morning."

"I'm sorry to startle you, dear," Estelle said with a smile. She wore a blue silk scarf around her head, tied just under her chin, but the outline of curlers was clear beneath the fabric. "I didn't expect anyone to be up at this time."

"You're up and about early." Isabella smiled as she held the front door for the old woman.

"Yes. I like to go to the grocery store at this time of day.

They're open twenty-four hours now, and it's so nice to shop without all the swarms of old folks filling the aisles. You would not believe how slow some of these people are! Standing for hours trying to figure out which loaf of bread is cheapest, while they're blocking the aisle with their cart. Then they all want to chitchat with me. I'm there to shop!" Estelle clucked her tongue and shook her head. "I like to go early to avoid all the old folks."

Isabella couldn't help but giggle as they made their way to the parking lot. "Perfectly understandable."

"But what are you doing here at this time, young lady?" Estelle asked, turning her head to eye Jace's window in the apartment building with unerring accuracy.

Feeling a flush of embarrassment, Isabella managed to hedge around the question. "I have to be into work early today."

"I see. So are you still playing the field?"

Playing the field wasn't exactly how Isabella would described her search for a man, but she didn't bother to correct the phrase. "I... I guess."

"Don't you know?"

"It's complicated."

"It's never as complicated as young people make it. Let me ask you this. What exactly do you want?"

It was the same question Jace had asked her a few hours ago, and Isabella answered it in much the same way. "I want a lot of things, but one of them is to get married and have a family."

Estelle nodded. They were standing next to the driver's

door of her big tank of a sedan, but she didn't get into it yet. Instead, she said, "Then my advice to you is not to settle for anything less."

"I'm... I'm not planning to."

"Good. Because that's not always the case, you know. I see so many young ladies just taking crumbs from young men because they're too afraid to insist on what they really want. And the young men just keep offering crumbs because they can get what they want without giving anything more. And how can you blame them? If they can get what's easy and fun without making any effort, then why would they step up?"

Isabella had always liked Estelle, but she'd always done so in a slightly amused way. She wasn't amused now though. The words hit her hard, in a way she hadn't expected. She swallowed. "I... yeah."

Estelle glanced back toward the window in Jace's apartment visible from the parking lot. "Don't settle for crumbs when you want the whole loaf of bread."

"I won't."

Jace had never offered Isabella nothing but crumbs. He'd always been so good and sensitive and generous. But maybe she was settling for them anyway because she was too confused and scared to really think through—or talk through—what she wanted.

Estelle reached out and patted Isabella on the arm. "I'm glad to hear it, dear."

That evening, Isabella dropped by Jace's apartment after work, determined to have a real conversation—the one they'd started the night before that had gotten interrupted.

Jace had obviously been working on a stool at the kitchen bar because his laptop and papers were spread out all over the granite counter. He pulled his glasses off as he let her into the apartment. "I wasn't expecting you so early," he said with a smile.

She smiled back. She'd been resolute before, but now that she saw him, all cute and rumpled and questioning, her throat started to tighten.

What was she thinking? What kind of guy would be happy about a girl showing up on his doorstep, insisting on having a state-of-the-relationship talk?

If Jace wanted more than sex from her, he would have told her.

He'd never lied to her before. He wasn't going to start lying to her now.

Her sisters were right. Jace had had years to tell her if he had the slightest interest in anything romantic with her. He obviously never had before. And if he was starting to now, he would have let her know. She'd given him a perfectly good opportunity to confess any growing feelings last night, and he'd made it clear that all he wanted was friendship and sex.

And that was fine. It was *fine*.

She wanted a husband, and that obviously was never going to be Jace.

It didn't have to be.

She could find someone else.

And if she couldn't at the moment imagine any other man knowing and caring for her the way Jace did, if she couldn't imagine wanting to open up her heart to any other man the way she did with Jace, and if she couldn't imagine enjoying sex more with any other man than she did with Jace, then eventually she would realize she was wrong.

She couldn't destroy her friendship with Jace. She just couldn't.

"What is it?" Jace asked, when she just stood there like an idiot.

She took a ragged breath, and the word that came out was, "Nothing."

He cocked his head and peered at her.

Afraid he would see some of what she was thinking, she put down her bag and took three steps closer so she could press herself against him. "I've just been wanting to do this all day."

It was true. She did want to kiss him. She did want him to start touching her.

And that was so much safer than pressing an issue that might blow up in both their faces.

He chuckled and took her head in both his hands, kissing her until she was breathless. "Me too."

After a few minutes, Jace carried her over to the couch, pulling up her skirt so she could wrap her legs around him and he could sink inside her.

They made love like that, urgent and mostly dressed, until both of them had reached climax. Afterward, they lay together on the couch, wrapped up in each other. And Isabella tried to assure herself that everything was fine.

This was just a phase they were going through. Eventually they'd have to stop having sex, and they could go back to being friends the way they were.

The worst thing she could do was put pressure on Jace and make him think she wanting more from him. That was the one thing that would definitely ruin their friendship for good.

Jace didn't want her that way.

If he did, he would have told her.

He'd always been honest with her.

She could trust him completely, and he would have told her if he wanted more from their relationship.

She needed to stop stressing about this and just accept the world the way it was. Jace was her friend. Some other man would have to be her husband.

"Idiot," a voice burst out from the corner of the living room. "Idiot!"

She gasped and stretched her neck to see Beau glaring at them from his cage.

"Idiot!" Beau squawked again.

Relieved at the distraction, Isabella giggled. "What have you been teaching him to say?"

"I haven't taught him anything," Jace replied in a dry, aggrieved voice. "He just gets a word in his head and keeps saying it."

"But why have you been calling him an idiot? He's really very smart."

"I haven't been calling him an idiot."

She stroked his back, under his shirt. She loved the feel of his warm, firm skin. "Then who have you been calling an idiot? He's obviously heard you say it."

For a moment, Jace was very still. Then he laughed and sat up, pulling his pants back up and fastening them. "Maybe I've mentioned it to him a time or two."

"Well, you need to be nicer to him. He's a very smart little fellow."

"Fell-o. Fell-o. Idiot!"

She laughed and smoothed down her skirt.

"You want to hang out this evening?" Jace asked. "We could do dinner or..."

She sighed and shook her head. It was exactly what she wanted to do, but she knew it would be a mistake. She couldn't start feeling too domestic with Jace. Having sex. Making dinner. Going to sleep together. That would be the most dangerous thing she could do to her own feelings. "I better not. I told my mom I'd come over and help her clean out her refrigerator."

"Sounds like an exciting evening."

"It will be okay. She usually gives me all the cookies and fudge she's been hoarding, so it's worth it."

"Well, give me a call later on."

"I will." She stood up, feeling slightly sore and quite debauched after having a quickie on the couch the way they just had.

She'd never felt debauched before. It was an entirely new feeling.

But not really a bad one.

She was pulling into her parents' driveway when her phone rang. She grabbed it, thinking it might be Jace.

When she saw it was Cliff, she felt a drop of her heart.

She shouldn't be disappointed. They'd had a decent date, and she'd been kind of surprised when he hadn't called her back. But here he was calling after all.

She had more potential for a future with Cliff than with Jace. She needed to accept that and move on.

She connected the call and greeted him with a little small talk. Then he asked, "Are you busy tonight? I thought we could maybe grab a cup of coffee if you're interested."

"Well, I was actually going to help my mom clean her refrigerator."

Cliff laughed. "Is that an excuse? I'm sorry I didn't call before, but I've been out of town."

She should be excited. He hadn't been blowing her off. He was interested in her. He was a good guy, a good catch.

Good potential.

Way more potential than Jace.

"It wasn't an excuse. It was the truth. But I'm sure my mom won't mind waiting until tomorrow. Where did you want to meet?"

An hour later, she was heading to a coffee shop in town to meet Cliff, telling herself over and over again that this was for the best.

Coffee with Cliff might turn into something else, and they'd all be happier that way.

12

————

IT WASN'T OFTEN THAT JACE FOUND HIMSELF WALKING around town on his own. Isabella or maybe one of his co-workers was normally with him. But after Isabella had left him earlier, he had felt unsettled and more than a little hungry. Dinner seemed like the logical choice, but he had nothing at home that interested him, and all the good places didn't deliver.

So there he was. Walking around town. Alone.

It wasn't so bad. It wasn't as if he was walking around with a neon sign announcing he was a loser. He waved to Mr. Martin, who owned the hardware store. Then he smiled and said a quick hello to Mrs. Jennings, who worked as a cashier at the diner. Just as he was about to cross the street, he spotted a familiar figure.

Isabella.

Only she wasn't alone.

What the...

Jace froze in his tracks as he zeroed in on who was with her, and he felt like he might be sick.

Cliff.

She'd just left his bed—well, his couch—and immediately afterward she went out on a damn date with Cliff?

What the hell?

A car approaching had him jumping back on the sidewalk, and luckily there was a tree that he could step behind to make sure Isabella and Cliff didn't see him. Cliff was holding the door of the coffee shop open for her, and she smiled at him as she walked inside.

Now what? What was he supposed to do? Stand there and watch them through the window? Keep track of how long they stayed inside? Or was he supposed to storm across the street and demand that she leave with him?

"Jace?"

He turned and spotted one of his neighbors, Chris, walking toward him with a smile on his face. Sure. And why wouldn't Chris be smiling? He was engaged to Heather, the woman of his dreams, and they were planning their wedding and almost too happy to be around.

Not that Jace would admit that to his friend.

"Hey, Chris," he said casually. "What's up?"

Chris looked at him and then across the street, to the tree and then back to Jace. "Are you hiding from someone?"

"What?" Jace croaked. He cleared his throat. "I mean, uh, no. I was... I was just trying to decide where I wanted to grab some takeout from, that's all."

The look on Chris's face showed that he didn't really believe him. "And you were thinking of the coffee shop? Because if you were, I can offer some other suggestions that would be a lot better."

Jace chuckled and shook his head. "No. I'm good. Really. I just saw... I mean, I noticed..."

"Isabella?"

Shit. Why deny it?

"Yeah."

Chris nodded, his expression surprisingly understanding for such a no-nonsense guy. "Things okay with you two?"

"Honestly? No."

"Want to talk about it?"

Did he? Not particularly. And especially not here on the street. "Thanks, but not really."

Chris nodded again. "I get it. But you helped me when I was in a bad way, so if I can help at all..."

"I appreciate that."

They stood there for a minute, and then Chris straightened and let out a breath. "Well I need to go. I'm picking up some Chinese for me and Heather. Which, by the way, would be my recommendation for you as well. I'll see you around."

At first Jace didn't say anything. He just waved. But then he heard himself asking, "Hey, Chris?"

"Yeah?"

"When Heather was dating other guys—you know, before the two of you hooked up—did it bother you?"

Raking a hand through his hair, Chris looked around and then walked back over to Jace. "Yeah, it bothered me. It bothered me a lot. I even tried sabotaging some of her dates." He paused, and then it was as if a switch was flipped. "Oh, that's it. Isabella's out with someone, isn't she?"

Jace nodded. "At the coffee shop."

"And?"

"And it's pissing me off," Jace admitted reluctantly. He didn't want to admit to everything he and Isabella had been doing, but he really needed some input to help him keep his shit together. "Let's just say that I thought things were... progressing between the two of us, and then I find her going out with this guy."

"I see."

"So what am I supposed to do? It's not like we're a couple or anything, but—"

"But you want to be."

"Yeah. Pretty much."

"And does she know this?"

"I thought she did. But now? I guess not."

"Dude, you've got to talk to her about it. Don't go on the attack or anything. Maybe invite her to dinner—something casual—and just... lay it out there. You guys have been friends for too long to screw things up with jealousy. If you've got feelings for her—and I know you do—then stop waiting around. Tell her."

He let out a ragged sigh. Chris was right. It was time. He couldn't go on like this. *They* couldn't go on like this.

"Thanks. You're right. I'm gonna do it. Tonight."

Chris smiled and nodded. "Good. Keep me posted."

"I will. Now go and get your Chinese food and tell Heather I said hello."

"Will do." This time when Chris turned and walked away, Jace let him. He turned and focused his attention on the coffee shop again.

He couldn't just walk over, barge in, and invite her to dinner. That would just be awkward. And clearly she had lied to him about going to her parents' house, so...

Before he could second-guess himself, he pulled out his phone and started typing.

In town. Saw you at the coffee house. I'm picking up Chinese. Dinner at 7. We need to talk.

He hit send before he could second-guess himself. He knew Isabella well enough to know she would read his text and not question it or try to back out. Not now that she knew she'd been caught in a lie.

Sliding the phone back into his pocket, he looked around and went to step out from behind the tree when he saw something crawl across his shoe.

A spider.

Without much thought, he stomped on it.

"Isabella's not here, Jace. You could have let that one live."

He looked up and saw Elise walking by with an armload of shopping bags and a big smile on her face.

"Just practicing!" he called out.

And with a lightness he couldn't believe he felt, he turned and made his way to the Chinese restaurant.

At two minutes after seven, there was a knock at his door. Jace took a steadying breath and opened it. If anything, Isabella looked just as nervous as he felt.

"Hey," she said quietly, clutching the strap to her purse in her hands.

"Hey. C'mon in."

She stepped around him and walked right into the center of the living room—as if putting as much space between them as she could. Closing the door, Jace walked over to the kitchen table and motioned for Isabella to join him.

"Harder!" Beau squawked out.

Isabella gasped, her eyes going wide and her cheeks growing red.

Jace chuckled nervously. "Just... ignore him. He's a damn nuisance."

"Isn't Erin supposed to be back by now?"

"They're staying longer than they planned. I'd sure like a job where I could take such a long vacation." He was grumbling, mostly as a way of filling the awkward space between them.

"Blue dress!" the bird called out.

Jace groaned and tried to divert Isabella's attention to

the food. He'd gotten all their usual favorites—sesame chicken, Hunan shrimp, beef lo Mein and a couple of egg rolls. When Isabella walked over, he noticed that she wouldn't meet his gaze directly. For now, he'd let that go. They'd eat first. Then he'd do his best to get to the bottom of whatever it was that they were doing in this relationship.

No sooner had he started dishing out the food than Isabella started to speak.

"Were you spying on me?" she asked with a bit of defensiveness.

"Excuse me?"

"You heard me. You didn't mention that you were going in to town when I left here earlier. I thought you were going to be at a poker game. Then you just *happen* to see me at the coffee shop? Seriously?"

A mirthless laugh escaped before he could stop it. "Funny, when you left here, you said you were going to your parents' house and yet somehow ended up having coffee with Cliff." He did his best to keep his tone level and to not add to an already-volatile situation by raising his voice.

Isabella put a few items on her plate but simply pushed them around with her fork rather than eating. "I did go to my parents, but Cliff called and... I don't know. I just figured I'd go and meet him for coffee. It seemed like the thing to do."

Jace saw red.

The thing to do? What the hell did that mean? Which

was exactly what he demanded, standing up from his chair.

She looked up at him with wide eyes. "I don't see what the big deal here is or why you're so surprised." She jumped to her feet as well. "I never lied to you, Jace. Not once! All this time you knew what I was looking for! What I wanted!"

"Earlier today you wanted me!"

That little outburst seemed to shock them both. For a long time they stood breathless and stared at one another.

For the life of him, Jace wasn't sure what to do or say next. Was she going to deny what she felt—what they'd been doing—and why?

Her silence just seemed to rile him up even more. "How is it that you can go from my bed to a date, Bella, huh?" He took a step toward her. "How can you possibly do that? Does what we have mean nothing to you?"

"I... it wasn't... you said nothing was going to change!" She'd raised her voice now too. "I told you it would! Sex always does. We never fought before. We never had this kind of awkwardness between us. Now look at us!"

He was ready to yell something back, but the catch in her voice stopped him. Isabella turned her back on him, and he could see her trembling. Not once in all their years of friendship had he ever been able to handle her tears.

He still couldn't.

Stepping forward, Jace put his hands on her shoulders and went to turn her around, but she jerked out of his grasp. When she faced him, her eyes were wet with tears. "I can't do this anymore, Jace. I thought I could. I really, really did. And... and... I won't settle for crumbs. I need more."

"Crumbs? What are you—"

"I've just been taking what I can get, but it's not enough for me. And now everything is ruined."

"Okay, okay... let's just try to calm down. I think—"

"No! You don't you get it. Everything has changed. It's ruined! And now I'm not sure I can even just hang out with you anymore!"

Panic gripped him by the throat. "Don't say that!"

"But what if it's true? I come over here, and all I can think about is how much I want you and—"

"Say it again," he said, his voice husky and thick.

Isabella blinked at him as if she didn't quite understand what he had said.

"Say it, Bella."

He saw her swallow hard. "Say what?" she asked, her voice still a little shaky.

"Say that you want me."

This was it. The make-or-break moment. They had rarely talked in the heat of passion before. But now he needed the words. He wanted to say them to her as well.

"Bella."

"I want you," she whispered, so soft that he almost didn't hear her.

Reaching out, his hand wrapped around her nape, and he roughly pulled her toward him. "Again."

"I want you." Her voice was stronger this time.

"God, Bella. You have no idea what hearing you say that does to me."

"Show me."

They'd had sex on the floor, on the couch, against the wall, and right now he was ready to add kitchen table to their repertoire, but rather than pounce, he opted to seduce.

Leaning forward, he trailed kisses from her temple, down across her cheek, her jawline and her throat. He gently bit where her pulse was rapidly beating and felt her shudder against him. The feel of her body against his was like hitting the launch button. He was already hard and primed, and it took every ounce of willpower to do this right.

While he continued to kiss and nip at her soft skin, he told her what he wanted to do. "I'm going to show you all night long how much I want you, sweet Bella," he murmured. "I'm going to take my time and touch every beautiful inch of you." Then he raised his head. "If you'll let me."

Isabella licked her lips and nodded, her eyes glazed and clouded with passion. She was sexy as hell, and she didn't even realize it.

Taking her by the hand, he led her to his bedroom and said a silent prayer of thanks that it was relatively clean. Together they moved as if choreographed toward the bed. Isabella sat, and then Jace followed her down, stretching out beside her.

His hands never stopped moving. His lips were never

far from her delectable mouth. He had her naked in moments, and then he took his time looking at her—all of her. The sight of her sprawled out just for him stole his ability to speak.

And speaking was highly overrated when all he wanted to do was touch her, taste her.

And he did.

"Jace!" she cried out as he sucked gently on one hardened nipple and then the other. One large hand splayed across her belly as he suckled her. Isabella's breath was ragged as she writhed against him. "More. I want more."

There was no way he was moving away from her breasts just yet, so he let his hand skim down until he was cupping her and smoothly inserting one finger, then two, inside her. Isabella's back arched off the bed, and he felt a sense of pure male pride that he could bring this kind of a reaction out in her.

By now he knew what she liked, knew how he would make her come. But he wasn't ready for that yet. He wanted to tease her, touch her, play with her.

Isabella's head thrashed from side to side as Jace's fingers teased in and out of her. He knew she was getting close. He honed in on her clit and applied just enough pressure to send her soaring. She cried out his name, and he immediately crushed her mouth with his, swallowing her cries, her pleas, even as he cursed the fact that he was still dressed.

Lucky for him, Isabella was on the same page, and together they worked on getting him naked.

And fast.

No sooner had his boxers hit the floor than he was watching as Isabella slid a condom on him. God, he loved how her hands felt around him—so soft, so sure... so damn good.

"Now, Bella," he growled, covering her body with his. "I need to be in you right now."

And with a sexy smile, she lay back and spread her legs in invitation.

So. Damn. Hot.

The instant he slid into her wet heat, he groaned with satisfaction. "So tight, Bella. I love how tight you are around me."

"You feel so good," she purred, wrapping her legs around him. "So deep. So, so deep..."

Somewhere in the back of his mind, Jace knew he'd wanted to go slow, but he couldn't. Didn't even want to anymore. He needed to move—to claim. They found their rhythm, and she met him thrust for thrust. Their breaths mingled, tongues tangled as they moved together. It just kept getting better and better. Nothing would ever feel as good as Isabella wrapped snugly around him as she panted his name.

He loved how she felt.

He loved the things she said.

He loved... her.

So much so that it hurt.

"Yes, Jace... just like that. It's so good. So good. I love it," she said in a breathy tone.

He knew he was close, but he needed her to come again. Gently, he nipped on her earlobe. "Come for me, sweet Bella. Come for me, baby." Shifting positions slightly, adjusting his angle, he knew the instant he hit her clit in just the right way.

"That's it... right there... oh, oh, oh!" She clamped tight around him as she came. She made needy sounds. She clutched at him. "Yes, yes, yes... God, I love it... I love it..."

And then he was there. His body tightened as he came in a hot rush inside her. "I love you, Bella! I love you so much," he gasped out as he emptied into her. "I always have, baby... always... always."

13

Isabella's mind was filled with such a rush of pleasure, joy, and satisfaction that she couldn't do anything but gasp as she tried to recover from the intensity of their lovemaking.

She felt so incredibly good. All over. Body and heart.

Like finally everything about her world had put itself together.

Jace wanted her too. Every bit as much as she wanted him.

He cared about her in exactly the same way she cared about him.

That much had been more than clear in the way he'd taken her just now. All the details were a blur, but she at least knew that much.

Nothing else really mattered.

At least, not right now.

Jace was just as breathless as he took care of the

condom and then pulled her into his arms under the covers. She pressed herself against him, loving the feel of his warm body.

Loving everything about him.

He was Jace, and there was no other Jace in the world.

She couldn't think clearly enough to even speak, but it felt like they didn't need to.

For the moment, everything was perfect, and she could rest in that knowledge, in that peace.

She fell asleep after just a few minutes.

She woke up briefly once or twice, but only long enough to cuddle up against Jace again and drift back off to sleep.

It was still dark in the room. He was sleeping too, and there was no reason yet to wake up.

The next time she woke up, light was coming in from around the edges of the blinds. She blinked at the clock until she could read that it was almost seven in the morning.

Still early. She didn't have to get moving quite yet.

With a sigh of satisfaction, she rolled over so she was facing Jace. His eyes were still closed, and he looked so peaceful, like he was sated, like he was just as happy as she was, even in his sleep.

She smiled as she played out the details of the evening before, thrilling over the memory of the words he'd said, the ways in which he'd touched her.

All was good until her memory made it to the climax. He'd said something as he'd come. It was a blur of heat and pleasure, since she'd just come herself, but there was something about it, something significant...

She frowned as she tried to remember exactly what he'd said.

He'd said he loved her.

Her heart leaped in excitement at the knowledge.

She loved him too. She always had, and it seemed inevitable, so right, that their love should have transformed into something else over the past few weeks.

But that wasn't all he had said.

He'd said more.

He loved her. Always had. Always had.

She sat up in bed as the memory tightened into clarity.

Maybe he'd meant he'd always loved her as a friend—the way she'd loved him—but now that she was hearing him rasp out the words again, she somehow knew he meant differently.

She'd assumed his feelings had changed the way hers had, but evidently they hadn't.

Had he loved her all this time?

Had he wanted her all this time?

Had he kept it a secret from her, never telling her something that went so deep, something she really needed to know?

She tried to breathe slowly, think clearly, work things out in a rational way.

But there was no rationality that could overcome the sudden wave of grief and betrayal that swept over her.

Suddenly, all his strange behavior over the past couple of weeks made sense.

He'd loved her all this time. He hadn't wanted her to date anyone but him.

All this time he'd been pretending to be supportive when he was really keeping secrets from her.

Lying to her.

Jace. Whom she'd trusted more than anyone. Whom she'd foolishly believed would never deceive her.

She was almost choking as she scrambled out of bed, searching the floor for her clothes and grabbing them as she stumbled toward the front door of the apartment.

There was no way she could be reasonable about this. She might as well try to be reasonable about the ground opening up beneath her.

There was no logic to make it go away.

The only thing left to do in the face of this kind of crumbling foundation was to run.

She was mostly dressed as she hurried down the hallway and out of the building. It was a beautiful day, and the sunrise was casting a lovely orange shading onto the world.

Isabella couldn't appreciate it though. She half walked, half ran toward the parking lot.

Her car was there. Her car could take her away.

Maybe then she could think, figure out what was

happening here, figure out how she was supposed to react to Jace betraying her trust the way he had.

She was so blinded by emotion that she almost ran into a young woman walking toward her on the sidewalk, carrying a large box.

The near collision caused the woman to jerk, and the box started to slide out of her hands.

Reacting instinctively, Isabella reached out to grab the box so it didn't fall sideways onto sidewalk and spill out all its contents.

"Oh, thank you," the woman said with a slightly hassled smile. "That thing weighs a ton."

The woman was very pretty, with a sweet face, red hair, and a dimple on the right side of her mouth. Isabella had never seen her before.

"Are you moving in?" she asked, glad of the momentary distraction from the heartache that seemed to be waiting for her behind a door in her mind that was about to be ripped open.

"Yes," the woman said. "I'm Daisy. It's nice to meet you."

Daisy's smile was so warm and sincere that Isabella tried to smile back. "I'm Isabella. I don't live in the building but my... my friend... does."

She hated stumbling over the word. Jace had been her friend for so long.

In what kind of world would that no longer be true?

Daisy's smile faded as she looked at Isabella's face. "Are you okay?"

Nodding, Isabella tried again to smile. "Yeah. Yeah, I'm fine." It felt like her eyes were burning as she thought about Jace back in the apartment.

He would wake up to find her gone.

She couldn't stand the idea of it.

But she just had to get away so she could think.

"I'm sorry," Daisy murmured, obvious sympathy on her face. "I'll let you go. I need to hurry anyway. My dad's coming over in a few hours to move me in, and I want to have most of the boxes done by then. He thinks I can't do anything on my own, so I'd like to prove him wrong." She was smiling again as she leaned back down to pick up the box.

Isabella was faintly interested in this piece of information and wondered what Daisy's family was like. But she didn't have the emotional energy to dwell on it at the moment. "Good luck," she said, as she started walking toward her car.

She'd reached the driver's side door when a voice called out from behind her. "Bella! Bella, *wait!*"

She knew who it was, of course.

Jace.

She turned her head to see him running down the front steps. He wore nothing but a pair of sweats. Not even any shoes.

She probably would have had time to get into the car and put it into drive before he reached her. She could have escaped from this conversation.

But that felt weak. And like a betrayal.

She didn't want to do that to him.

So she took a deep breath and turned to face him, her back to her car. She was trembling when he reached her.

"What's the matter?" he demanded, breathless, his eyes searching her face anxiously. "Why are you leaving like this?"

He would know that something was wrong. She never would have left without a word otherwise.

She tried to say something, but the words caught in her throat. She made nothing but a strangled sound.

Jace's features twisted. "Bella, baby, what's the matter?"

Her head jerked to the side at the hoarse endearment.

She loved when he called her that, but it was wrong.

It was wrong.

All this was wrong now, when she'd thought last night it felt so right.

"You..." She had to clear her throat and start again. "You said you loved me."

Jace's face changed as enlightenment evidently dawned in his mind. "Oh."

"Did you mean it?"

There was a moment's pause before he admitted softly, "Yes. I did. I love you."

She took a ragged breath. "You said... you said you always have... loved me. Did you mean that too?"

Another pause before he said, "Yes. I meant it. I've always loved you."

Her heart should be bursting with joy at the words, but

it wasn't. It felt frozen, constricted, in her chest. "And you never told me?"

Jace opened his mouth, but this time didn't say anything. He just shook his head.

"You lied to me?"

"I didn't lie to you, Bella. I just—"

"You did lie. You've been keeping this secret, and you never admitted it, even when we were talking about all kinds of things that... that mattered. You were deceiving me about your feelings. Don't you dare say that you weren't." The tears that had been trapped in her eyes were starting to stream down her face now.

She couldn't help it. Couldn't stop it.

"Oh, baby," Jace murmured, reaching out to brush them away. "Please don't cry. I did keep the secret, but I didn't know what else to do."

His voice was so gentle, so full of feeling, that she wanted to hear more of it. She found herself leaning her face into his hand, wanting his touch on her skin.

"You didn't love me back," he continued. "What was I supposed to do?"

She jerked away from him as she once again realized the reality. "You could have told me! Why didn't you tell me?"

"How was I supposed to tell you?" Jace asked, rubbing his face with what looked like frustration. "First, you were with Brock. And then I—"

She gasped with another surge of pain and betrayal. "Since Brock? You've had feelings for me since Brock? So...

all this time... our whole friendship... none of it has been real?"

"Of course it's been real!" He sounded a little rougher now. Maybe just desperate. "Everything has been real between us."

"Except it hasn't been—not if you've been hiding this secret from me. How could you have..." She couldn't say anything more as sobs started to rip through her throat.

"Oh, baby. Please don't." He reached out toward her.

She jerked away.

Jace's shoulders slumped, as if he were finally realizing how serious, how intense, her response was to learning the truth. "I understand if you're hurt, but can we at least talk about it?"

She shook her head through her tears. "Not now. I can't talk now."

"Then when? We can't just throw everything away because you're upset about this."

Somehow he was making it sound like this was her fault. Like he'd done nothing wrong and she was being irrational.

It made everything hurt even more.

She swiped her tears away and glared at him. "Don't you dare make it sound like I'm in the wrong here. You're the one who lied! You're the one who's been lying all this time!"

He started to answer and then stopped. Cleared his throat. "You're right. I did. And I'm sorry it's hurt you so much. But we still need to talk about it."

"We can later. But not right now. I can't even think right now." She fumbled until she'd found her keys in her purse.

She hadn't yet found them when something caught her attention at the front of the apartment building. It looked like a blue and green streak flying out of the entrance.

Behind it came running a tiny Yorkie, yapping at the top of her little voice.

She recognized the dog. Lucy. Chris and Heather's Yorkie. But what was she chasing?

She stared in a daze as the brightly colored streak ended up in a big tree on the front lawn, with Lucy barking her head off on the grass beneath.

"Is that Beau?" Isabella breathed, walking over toward the tree without thinking, her keys still in her hand.

Jace hadn't been looking in the same direction, but he turned and followed her over, and they both stood near the yapping dog, staring up at Beau perched on a large branch of the tree.

"How did he get out?" Isabella asked breathlessly. "Did you leave the door open when you ran after me?"

"Damn, I must have." He grimaced, still staring up at the bird. "What if he just flies away? Erin will never forgive me."

"Here, Beau!" Isabella called, completely focused now on the crisis. She held out her hand, vaguely praying that the bird would come to her and perch on it. "Here, Beau! Come back to us! This little dog isn't going to hurt you."

Ignoring this slight to her canine dignity, Lucy kept barking in ferocious little yips.

"Come on back, Beau," Jace said soothingly, very slowly approaching the tree. "Please don't fly away. You're not really a bad fellow, and we'd miss you if you were gone."

Lucy kept barking her head off.

"Oh, be quiet!" Isabella instructed the dog, afraid Beau would never come down as long as the dog was present. "Nobody is afraid of you!"

"Lucy! Lucy, come!" A new voice broke into the morning, and Chris appeared at the entrance of the building, half-dressed and running down the steps. "You ungrateful scaredy-cat! I was just going to trim your claws!"

Relieved that one of the dog's owners was coming to claim the escapee, Isabella cooed up at Beau again, begging him to come down.

Beau had evidently been sizing up the situation and had come to his own conclusions. Before Jace could reach him, the bird dove down toward Lucy.

The dog squealed dramatically and staged an immediate retreat, racing back toward the building so fast she almost tripped on her own paws.

Beau was still chasing the dog when the Lucy reached Chris, leaping up into his arms for protection.

His vindication accomplished, Beau gave a few loud squawks and circled back to perch on Jace's shoulder.

Jace cringed as the claws must have dug in, but Isabella released a long sigh of relief.

She'd actually grown quite fond of the bird, and she would have hated for him to get lost.

Plus Jace and his sister would have been devastated.

"Sorry," Chris called out, petting the tiny dog who was trying to burrow into his chest. "She has delusions of grandeur."

"It's fine," Jace said, keeping his hand on Beau so the bird wouldn't fly away again. "We got him. No harm done."

Chris waved to them as he carried the dog back into the building, warning the dog of punishment coming in the form of trimmed claws.

Isabella had been smothering a laugh at the sight of Beau chasing the dog away, and she smiled over at Jace.

He smiled back, and they shared a brief look that was warm, affectionate, completely understanding.

Then she remembered what had happened, how their friendship had been cracked in two.

Emotion strangled in her throat as she turned her face away from him.

Jace gave an audible sigh. "I'm so sorry, Isabella."

"I know," she managed to say.

"We do need to talk."

The brief distraction had totally dissipated now, and Isabella was on the verge of tears again. "Later," she managed to say. "I just... can't now."

Jace stood watching her, perfectly still, perfectly silent. It was like a coil of deep emotion was trapped inside him somewhere, but he'd clamped down on it so powerfully it couldn't escape. "Okay," he said at last. "We can talk later. When do you think—"

"I don't know. I don't know. You have to give me some time."

"Okay." She could hardly recognize his hoarse voice. "Okay."

Isabella stared at her best friend for a long moment, Beau on his shoulder, wondering if she'd ever really known him at all.

"Okay," Jace said one more time. "Drive safe."

She nodded, finally feeling free to return to her car and drive away.

As she was turning onto the street, she saw Daisy come back out of the building. The other woman paused, evidently seeing how upset Isabella was. Daisy gave her a little wave and a deeply sympathetic smile, a silent acknowledgement of understanding and empathy.

It made Isabella cry again—that a stranger could be so sweet when her best friend hadn't ever been open or truthful with her.

She pulled out onto the street and drive toward her own apartment, aware the whole time that Jace was standing in the parking lot like a statue, watching her drive away.

14

—————

A WEEK.

He'd given her a week.

She hadn't returned any of his calls, and whenever he'd shown up at the shop, she had hid in the back. Yeah, he knew she was hiding, but he didn't want to cause a scene.

Now he did.

Now that was all he wanted to do. He was going to make her face him—once and for all—and hear him out. It was a Saturday, so he knew she'd be at work and that it would be so busy that she couldn't possibly go and hide. All he had to do now was figure out what he was going to say to make her listen.

Actually, he'd been working on it all week, but now that he was primed and ready to go, it seemed... lame. Not enough. Jace first thought of doing the overly romantic gestures—going to her with flowers and candy and jewelry

—but he knew that those weren't the things that would matter to Isabella. Then he thought about going to her and reading romantic lines of poetry. That thought was instantly squashed when he tried doing it and realized that he didn't understand what most of them meant and that using someone else's words wouldn't impress her anyway.

So his next thought was to simply speak from the heart.

But there weren't enough words for him to convey all that she was to him, and he ended up stammering and stumbling to get the words out.

Inspiration had hit while flipping through the channels late one night and seeing the movie *Love Actually*. The scene where the guy stood outside the girl's door and used those giant cards to say how he felt? It was perfect.

Except he remembered Isabella making him watch that movie years ago and commenting on while that scene was sweet, it was also a cowardly way to tell someone how you feel.

And he was back to the drawing board.

Dammit.

What was he supposed to do?

With a loud sigh, he went about his morning routine—had a cup of coffee and let Beau out to fly around. His eyes rolled as he thought about the bird and made a mental note to strangle his sister for leaving him here for so damn long! Granted, she had a good reason—vacation and... wait a minute, why was the damn bird still here?

Jace reached for the phone and pulled up his sister's number.

"Hey, there!" Erin said cheerily when she answered.

"Why is this bird still here?" he snapped, willing to forgo a friendly greeting and get right to the point.

"We've been away, Jace."

"Yeah, I know, but now you're back," he reminded her. "You need to come and get him. Like today. Now, preferably."

Erin chuckled. "Oh, stop. You know he hasn't been that bad."

"He also hasn't been that great. I'm just... I'm done. Can you please come and get him today?"

Erin was silent for a minute. "What's going on? You're all snappish and pissy. Something wrong?"

Where did he even begin? Nowhere, actually. There was no way he was going to talk to his sister about what was going on with Isabella. Although there was a possibility that she could lead him in the right direction on how to win her back—or just win her. At all.

"Okay, can I ask you something?"

"Of course!" she said happily, clearly thrilled that he was going to confide in her.

"If you and Dale had a fight or a misunderstanding, and it was mostly his fault, what would you want him to do to prove to you that he was sorry?"

She went silent again.

"You know what? Never mind. It's not a big deal. I was just curious and—"

"I didn't even know you were dating anyone," Erin cut in.

"What? I mean, why would you think that?"

"Oh, please. Don't be a dufus. You don't ask a question like that when you're referring to a disagreement with a friend," she said with a chuckle. "So who is she? Anyone I know?"

Shit. "Never mind. I'll figure it out on my own."

"Is it Isabella?" she asked hopefully.

"Uh, what?" he croaked. "Bella? Why would I need relationship advice about Bella?"

"Oh, Jace. Are you really still in denial? Would you please just admit that you're in love with that girl and put us all out of our misery?"

"What are you talking about?"

"Please, everyone knows that you're crazy for her! Honestly, I think the whole town has been waiting patiently for you to get up off your ass and do something. I thought for sure when she started this whole dating thing that you'd finally man up."

"So everyone in town knows I'm in love with Bella?"

"Ah-ha! I knew it! I knew you loved her!"

Dammit. He'd fallen for the oldest trick in the book on that one. "I didn't... I mean, I was just repeating—"

"Just stop it," she said, and he knew she was smiling. "Look, clearly it's Isabella that we're talking about, and you somehow screwed something up. Am I right?"

He sighed. "Yes."

"Does she know how you feel?"

"Yup."

"And she doesn't feel the same way?"

"That's just it, I don't know how she feels—other than being pissed at me."

"Why is she pissed? How could you have screwed this up? The two of you are closer than any two people I know!"

"She's upset because I... I've felt this way for so long and never said anything about it. She feels like I've lied to her."

"Well, you really have."

"Not helping, Erin!" he snapped.

"Oh, sweetie. I don't even know what to say."

He was about to say something when suddenly inspiration struck. "You know what, you're brilliant!"

"What? I am? Why? What did I say? I don't remember saying anything!"

"Trust me. You said it all. I have to go. Come and get this bird! You have the spare key. Bye." He hung up and jumped up from the couch, spilling coffee on himself. "Damn!" But it didn't matter. He knew exactly what he was going to do to make things right with Isabella.

And after showering and getting dressed, he left his apartment and felt more hopeful than he could ever remember feeling.

∼

As predicted, the salon was mobbed. Every seat in the waiting area was full, and every chair at every station had a customer in it, and there were even a few people standing around and waiting.

Isabella's station was in the middle of the salon along the far wall, and as he approached the door, her back was to him. He pulled the door open, and the bell over it jingled, but the noise level was so high that he doubted anyone heard it. Stepping inside, he looked around and took a minute to just breathe.

His arms were empty—there weren't any flowers, candy, jewelry, or balloons—but his heart was full.

Jace couldn't say who spotted him first. All he knew was that all of a sudden, conversations started to die down, and the salon slowly quieted—with the exception of the radio playing in the background and the sound of Isabella talking to her client. She evidently noticed it and stopped cutting hair and looked around.

The moment her eyes met his, Jace sprang into action.

With a confidence he didn't fully feel, he straightened his posture and began to slowly walk toward her. "Isabella Warren," he began, loud enough that everyone in the salon could hear him, "you are my best friend. I can't remember a time when you weren't. You make me laugh, smile, think, and feel. You make my world a better place. I love spending time with you and talking with you and sharing our hopes and dreams with one another."

Isabella's arms dropped to her side, and her eyes went

wide as he got closer. She looked around nervously at first, but then it was as if she couldn't look away from him.

"But I screwed up. For all the things I shared with you, I didn't share the most important one—that I'm in love with you." There was a collective gasp throughout the salon, and he paused as murmurs followed. "I've been in love with you since the moment I met you, but you belonged to someone else. I was fine with us just being friends—as a matter of fact, I loved it. I loved that I got to see a side of you that most people don't see. I loved how you let your guard down and that we could just hang out together—because you wanted to and not because you had to."

"Jace," she began, but it was more of a "please stop doing this" rather than a "that's so sweet" sort of a thing.

But he wasn't deterred.

"I love that you enjoy eating an everything pizza with me and neither of us worry about garlic breath. I love that you laugh until you cry at even the lamest of jokes. I love that we can play board games at two in the morning just because we want to. I love hearing about your day and how when you ask about mine it's because you genuinely want to know."

By now he was standing less than a foot away from her. All around the room he heard comments like "I knew it!" and "How sweet!" and "It's about time!" But he hadn't heard anything from Isabella.

"Hearing your voice makes my day," he said, his voice a little softer now. "Seeing your face makes my heart beat faster. And kissing your lips—those sweet, sweet lips—is better than anything I've ever tasted in my life."

A small flush covered her cheeks, and Jace itched to reach out and touch them, but he knew he couldn't. Not yet.

"I should have told you," he said, his voice cracking a little. "I should have told you years ago how I felt. But you mean so much to me that I was afraid of losing you. You never gave me any indication that you thought of me as anything other than a friend." When Isabella went to correct him, he stopped her. "I'm not blaming you—the fault is completely mine. I wasn't brave enough. I wasn't confident enough. You see, I was willing to put my feelings aside in order to keep you in my life. I thought if you knew how I felt and you didn't feel the same way, that you'd walk away." He gave her a sad smile. "I can't imagine living my life without you in it, Bella."

Around them, you could have heard a pin drop.

When she continued to look at him but didn't respond, panic began its ugly path through him.

"Please don't make me live my life without you," he said, his voice gruff and raw.

Tears welled in her eyes, and it broke his heart. She couldn't turn him away, could she? She would forgive him. After all, he was done hiding and he was making it right—telling her exactly how he felt.

"I love you," he said, just in case he hadn't been clear. "I love you so much, and I don't think there will come a time when I'll ever stop loving you." He paused. "Tell me I'm not too late. Please."

Her head dropped forward, and her shoulders trembled as she took a shuddery breath. When she looked up at him, her tears fell.

"I'm so sorry," she said in a mere whisper.

Oh, God. This is what dying must feel like, he thought. Because she was truly killing him—ripping his heart out. "Bella—"

She shook her head. "I can't. I... I don't know how to move on from this. I don't know how to trust you."

"I didn't mean to—"

"But you did," she corrected, her voice growing a little stronger and then followed by more gasps from the people around them. "I'm still having a hard time processing that you've been lying all this time. I'm so sorry."

Her tears fell in earnest now, and at any other time, he would have felt free to reach out and wipe them away. But he couldn't now. He didn't have that right.

"I'm so sorry," she said one more time. "You need to go. Please."

There was one thing that he knew better than anything about Isabella—she didn't like to be pushed, and he'd pushed her enough for right now. Probably enough forever. It was over. They were over.

Jace couldn't speak, couldn't form a word even if he tried. With a curt nod, he turned and walked out of the salon.

And out of Isabella's life.

It was dark in his apartment, and Jace had to wonder when it had happened. He'd been home for hours and just sitting on his couch. Beau was gone and he was alone.

Something he had to get used to.

For the life of him, he couldn't remember driving home from the salon, but obviously he had. And now it was dark and lonely and pretty much how he viewed the rest of his life.

A knock on the door had him jumping up and foolishly believing it was Isabella. He nearly tripped over his own feet on his way to ripping the door open.

"Hey, man."

It was Chris.

Jace sagged against the door. "Oh, hey. What's up?"

"Heather was at the salon earlier, and she told me what happened. You okay?"

Jace motioned for Chris to come in. He flipped on the light switch to try to illuminate the place at least a little. When he shut the door and turn around, Chris was standing in the middle of the living room.

"Seriously, are you all right?" Chris asked.

All Jace could do was shake his head.

"She probably just needs a little time. I know when Heather and I first started, it was hard for her to accept that I really had feelings for her—that I really cared and had changed."

Jace sat down on the couch and sighed. "Bella and I

have known each other for so long, and she knows me, man. She... she knows me. I don't know why I didn't say something sooner. I should have. I freaking should have."

Chris sat down beside him. "Hindsight is always twenty-twenty." He paused. "You know you mean too much to her for the two of you to just... not see each other anymore, right? It's not possible."

"I'm tired of just seeing each other. I want more. I thought we were heading that way. And you know, I thought she was starting to feel more for me too. I had it all right within my reach, and I blew it."

But Chris shook his head. "You didn't blow it. You've just... given her a lot to think about. If you'd blown it, she would have fought you today in the salon. But she didn't. She cried, Jace. And I'm not saying that to make you feel bad but so you can see that there's hope."

Jace looked at Chris with disbelief. "Hope? You think making Bella cry gives me hope?"

A slow smile spread across Chris' face. "It should."

"Okay, I'll bite. Why?"

"She's crying because she cares, Jace. She's hurt and she's confused, but deep down she still cares. And she doesn't want to lose you."

"That's not the impression I got."

"You're not seeing what the rest of us are seeing," Chris countered. "Trust me. Give her a little more time."

"But what if... what if all she wants is to go back to being friends? I can't do that anymore. Not after knowing—"

"Yeah, I know. Believe me, I know. You've been patient all this time. Give her a little more of it. And then take it slow. Call her. Or text her. Maybe the two of you just need to ease back into things."

Maybe Chris was right, but it didn't make Jace feel any better. Right now he felt like his whole life was over. His chest ached, and it was like all the light and color was gone from his world.

Hell, right now he wouldn't even mind having Beau back. At least there'd be someone to talk to after Chris left.

"If you need anything," Chris went on, "I'm not far away. I'm serious—if you need to talk or want to go and grab a beer, just give me a call, okay?"

"Thanks."

15

ISABELLA STARED AT HERSELF IN THE BATHROOM MIRROR IN the salon, telling herself she'd made a huge mistake.

She had.

She couldn't get over how broken Jace had looked when she'd rejected him earlier that afternoon.

She shouldn't have done that.

No matter how hurt she still was about his hiding his feelings from her for so long, she never should have hurt him like that.

She'd always been so close to him that hurting him felt like a gaping wound in her own chest.

Releasing a shuddering breath, she glanced at her watch and straightened up at the time. Her last appointment of the day would be here soon. She needed to get out of the bathroom and face the world again.

She washed and dried her hands, although she hadn't actually used the bathroom, and then she made herself open the door and walk back to the front of the shop, where she saw Mrs. Pendergast was just arriving.

When the old woman saw her, she gave a warm smile. "Hello, dear. Thank you for fitting me in this late."

"Oh, it was no problem. How did your doctor's appointment go this morning?"

The next half hour was taken up with washing and rolling the woman's hair while hearing about the details of her appointment that morning. Isabella managed to smile and nod and make appropriate comments, but she was secretly praying that the hour would end soon so she could finally go home and have a good cry.

She was able to get away briefly as Mrs. Pendergast was sitting under the dryer, and when she returned the old woman was just hanging up her phone.

Elise had been working on a client's cut in the chair next to hers, but she glanced at Isabella as she walked back into the main room. Her rueful expression made it clear that something Isabella didn't want to happen was about to happen.

Mrs. Pendergast announced from under the dryer, "I just spoke with Gladys Hanes. Why didn't you tell me that young man declared himself this afternoon?"

Isabella's mood was so low she didn't think it could sink any further, but now it did. Gladys had been getting her nails done today when Jace had come in earlier.

"I'm sorry?" Isabella said, stalling as she walked over and raised the dryer, pretending to check whether Mrs. Pendergast's hair was appropriately dried.

It was, of course, and she had to fight the temptation to lower the dryer again over the woman's head and turn the heat up to high to drown out the conversation that was about to occur.

She resisted the temptation and switched off the dryer.

"That young man you're always attached to. He declared himself at last, didn't he?" Mrs. Pendergast got up and walked back over to Isabella's station.

Declared himself. That was one way to put it.

Isabella nodded and made a wordless affirmative sound, starting to unroll Mrs. Pendergast's hair. She didn't meet the other woman's eyes.

"So why aren't you riding off into the sunset with him right now?"

Isabella sighed and searched for something safe and yet still polite to say.

"Now Mrs. Pendergast," Elise said, shaking her head teasingly but obviously coming to the rescue. "We should try to give Isabella a little space."

"Why does she need space? Don't you care for the young man?"

"Of course I do," Isabella admitted. "But it's complicated."

"What's complicated? He's a good man and an excellent prospect. Why should it be complicated?"

"It's... it's hard... to trust in a relationship that isn't what he always pretended it was." Had she not been so drained emotionally, she never would have admitted something so private.

"What did he pretend it was?" Mrs. Pendergast demanded.

"Friendship."

"Not to interfere, since it's not really my business," Elise said, obviously speaking carefully so she wouldn't hurt or offend Isabella, "but aren't good romances based on friendship?"

"Maybe. Maybe. But—"

"He lied to you?" Mrs. Pendergast asked, narrowing her eyes as she studied Isabella's face in the mirror.

Isabella gave a little shrug. "He hid the truth from me."

"I see." Clearly thinking hard, the old woman evidently came to some sort of mental conclusion because her expression changed dramatically. "Then you were right to reject him. A liar is always going to lie, after all."

"Well, he didn't really lie," Isabella said, immediately jumping to Jace's defense.

"Didn't he? How often did he speak and act like he only wanted friendship from you?"

"I don't know. A lot."

"And how long did it go on?"

"Years," she admitted, dropping her eyes. "Since high school, I guess."

"Then there you have it. He's a liar who has been lying to you for years."

"He didn't think he could tell me. He didn't want to jeopardize our friendship. I can... I can understand that."

"Can you? Because I can't. A liar lies to take the easy way out, and that's what he did all this time."

"Maybe, but you should have seen him this afternoon. He put it all on the line. Risked everything. The whole town is going to know."

"The whole town probably already knows," Mrs. Pendergast said in a no-nonsense voice, "but that doesn't change the fact of him being a liar. You think he's going to change now? What else is he going to lie to you about?"

"He's never lied to me about anything else. And now the truth is out in the open. I can understand why he did what he did. I don't like it, but I can... can... under..."

She trailed off as she caught the expression on Mrs. Pendergast's face. Pleased. Victorious.

She'd done this whole thing on purpose—gotten Isabella to admit to herself that she could understand and sympathize with Jace's position.

Elise slanted her a little smile. "It sounds like you might have already forgiven him."

Isabella took a shaky breath. "Maybe. Maybe. I just don't know what to do."

"Maybe you should talk to him," Elise suggested.

"Yeah. Yeah. I guess I should. I just don't know what to tell him. My head is still spinning from everything. How am I supposed to figure it out?"

"Before I accepted Mr. Pendergast's proposal, I made sure he was the only man in the world I wanted to spend my life with."

"How did you do that?" Isabella asked, genuinely interested. Despite the old woman's meddling, she was clearly trying to help.

"I considered all the other possibilities, and that confirmed to me that no other man was at all acceptable to me."

Isabella drew her brows together. "How am I supposed to do that?"

"Oh, I know!" Elise explained. "I'm going to one of those speed dating things in Chester tonight. I'm trying to get back in the saddle after the divorce. You should come with me."

Isabella squeaked. "I don't want to do another speed dating thing! The last one was absolutely miserable."

"But how perfect would it be. It would be a shortcut to really seeing if there is any other man who has a chance to win your heart. It might help you really decide about Jace."

Isabella sighed. "But..."

"You should definitely do that," Mrs. Pendergast confirmed. "It's an excellent idea."

"Or you could go talk to Jace without really knowing how you feel. Do you want to do that to him?"

"No. I don't. Okay. I'll do it."

Four hours later, she was walking into a crowded room that was set up with small tables for the speed dating rounds.

She had no idea what she was doing here. She really wanted to go back to Preston and hang out with Jace.

Her sisters had all come over earlier to help her get

dressed and talk through the Jace situation. They'd all seemed to think the speed dating was an excellent idea—a chance for her to sort through her feelings.

It felt wrong. Ridiculous. Isabella shouldn't be here, sizing up all these men for potential dates.

Poor Jace was probably sitting all alone at home with a broken heart.

And Isabella had done it to him.

The idea of that was so painful that she couldn't stand it. As she was standing with Elise, waiting for the event to begin, she pulled out her phone and texted Jace.

Are you ok?

His reply came almost immediately. *Yes. What about you?*

I'm ok too. Are you sure you're ok?

I'll be fine. Don't worry about me.

It was such a Jace kind of response that her throat tightened. She was about to text again, but Elise was pulling her over to a seat at her assigned table and pushing her into it.

Isabella exhaled deeply as an announcer gave them directions and the event began.

The first man who came to her table wasn't bad-looking—balding but intelligent-looking. They made small talk about jobs and families for a few minutes, and Isabella didn't give him her card at the end of the conversation.

He seemed like a decent enough guy.

But he wasn't Jace.

In the time it took to shuffle tables, she texted quickly to Jace. *I'm sorry about this afternoon.*

Don't be. I was wrong. Not you.

In the middle of her response to his, the next man came to the table. He was attractive in a beefy way she didn't like, and he was also way too full of herself. She went through the motions of a conversation until their time was finally up.

In the next transition time, she finished her text to Jace. *I understand why you never said anything.*

And I understand why you're so hurt. It's my fault. Not yours.

She stared down at the words, wondering if there had ever been another man like Jace in the whole world.

The third man who came to her station was skinny and greasy and very awkward. Out of basic politeness, she managed through their entire allotted time, but she was immensely relieved to see him go.

As soon as she could, she replied to Jace's last message. *We should talk I guess.*

Any time. Whenever you're ready.

He was so sweet. And so sensitive. And so smart and understanding. He had such a warm heart. He was always so good to her.

No one had ever been so good to her.

Her next session passed in a blur. She couldn't remember anything about the man she talked to. Only that when it was finally over she could text back to Jace. *Can I come over tonight?*

Of course!

I'm stuck here for the moment but I'll come as soon as I can.

Her heart was racing, and she was breathing quickly as she went through the motions of three more sessions with men.

The event wasn't quite over when she finally couldn't take it anymore. She had to see Jace. Now.

She got up and was heading out the door during the next transition when Elise followed her, grabbing her arm. "Where are you going?"

"I can't do this anymore. I don't want any of these men. I want Jace."

Elise's face softened. "I know you do. But there's only two more sessions. You'll leave those poor guys hanging. Finish this up, and then you can go see him."

She shouldn't really worry about strangers she'd never met being left hanging, but she did. She'd always had a soft heart. So she relented and returned to her seat, where her next man was already waiting.

He was a bore who spent the whole time talking about gaming and comic books.

One more man now.

She just had to talk to one more man.

Then she could go be with Jace.

Maybe for the rest of her life.

She waited for her last man to appear, and was surprised when all the other guys were seated and he still hadn't appeared.

Maybe she was the one being left hanging—after she'd tried to be so nice.

Typical.

She was about to get up and leave when a man walked over and sat down across from her.

She stared, her mouth falling open.

Jace.

It was Jace.

Sitting right there across the table from her.

"What are you doing here?" she finally managed to ask.

He gave her a sheepish smile. "I... uh, well, they arranged it."

"They?"

"Everyone. Your sisters. Elise. Even old Mrs. Pendergast called me. Let me tell you, *that* was a disturbing conversation."

It took a moment, but the words finally sank in. As did the slight ironic twitch of Jace's mouth.

Isabella burst into laughter. "You're kidding!"

"No. I'm not. They said you... you were confused, but I needed to be available."

"And you weren't doing anything else tonight?"

He snorted. "Erin brought Beau back to keep me company. She said I needed the companionship more than she did. So I was sitting there talking to Beau. But everyone said they were sure you'd want to see me tonight."

"I do," she admitted, laughter now mixing with a deeper emotion, causing her eyes to burn. "I do, Jace. I'm so glad you're here."

"I'm glad too. I wouldn't have shown up here at this table, but it sounded like from your texts you were ready to talk."

"I am ready. I want to talk. I want to..." Her voice caught, and she had to swallow before she continued, "I want to do everything."

He met her eyes, hope springing to life there, even as she watched. "Do you really?"

"I do."

"So you didn't see any other guy here you want to date?"

"Not a single one."

"Just me?"

"Just you." She was close to tears as she smiled at him. "You're my last date of the evening—and maybe the last date of my life."

His expression broke in obvious relief, joy, love. "I'll work hard to make sure you never regret it."

"So can we get out of here now?"

"Yes. I think my speed dating days are over for good."

A few hours later, they were both in Jace's bed. His head was between Isabella's legs, and he was doing amazing things to her with his tongue and lips.

She was sobbing out a lot of loud, helpless sounds as an orgasm rose and broke inside her. She clutched at the headboard as she shook through the waves of pleasure, and she was smiling sappily down at Jace as she finally came down from the climax.

He was straightening up, clearly proud of himself for this accomplishment.

"Don't get smug," she told him, pulling him down into a hug. "I was just in desperate need of an orgasm. You weren't particularly skillful or anything."

Jace chuckled and brushed a kiss against her mouth. "Understood. No smugness from me."

He did look smug, but she didn't mind. She'd never been happier in her life.

When they'd gotten back to his apartment, she'd thought they were going to talk, but instead they started to kiss. Things had gotten urgent, and they'd ended up in the bedroom, making love with rough, naked passion.

They'd talked through things afterward, tangled up together under the covers.

They didn't come to any new revelations though.

They'd known each other for so long. They understood each other perfectly.

And now the one remaining wall between them had finally come down.

They loved each other all the way. Both of them knew it now.

"Are you hard again?" Isabella asked, when she felt his erection rubbing against her thigh.

"What do you think?" he asked hoarsely, moving over her and settling between her legs.

"And you think I'm up for another go?"

He smiled. "Are you?"

"I suppose I can muster the energy."

So he took her slowly, gently this time, and they rocked together in perfect unity, kissing deeply as both of them came to climax again.

She was tired—and utterly sated in a way she could never remember being before—when Jace finally rolled off her and pulled her against his side.

"I love you," he murmured, brushing his lips against her messy hair.

"I love you too."

"I can't believe this is really happening."

"Well, it is. And I think it's pretty great."

He chuckled. "Me too."

Isabella was about to drift off to sleep when she jerked in surprise at a loud squawk from the living room.

"Idiot! Idiot!" Beau declared to the world.

Isabella giggled. "He hasn't caught up to the most recent happenings with our relationship, I guess. We're not idiots anymore."

"He'll learn soon enough. He's pretty smart."

"Oh God!" Beau squawked. "God, God, God!"

Jace burst into laughter, as Isabella's cheeks burned with embarrassment, realizing when Beau had learned his latest vocabulary.

She must have been too loud in her vocal responses.

"I think he's caught up," Jace murmured, stroking her hair and her back.

"How long is Erin leaving him with you this time?"

Isabella demanded. "I hate to think what else he might learn to say."

"She's coming to get him tomorrow. He was just borrowed for the day, since I was so depressed. Honestly, I think I'm going to miss the old fella."

"Oh God! Idiot! Idiot!" Beau pronounced. "Oh God!"

Isabella giggled as Jace's arms tightened around her. "Or maybe not."

EPILOGUE

JACE PACED IN THE BACK ROOM OF THE BAR AND LOOKED AT his watch for the tenth time in five minutes. He hated relying on other people, but there was no other way for this to play out and be what he had worked out in his mind.

It was going to be perfect.

If he could get over his own anxiety and get his sister to be on time for once.

Peeking through the door, he almost sagged to the floor with relief. They were there.

A smile tugged at his lips as he saw Erin and Isabella walk through the door and then the look of utter confusion on Isabella's face. This was the bar where they had first speed dated. It was set up for that again, only this time each table had people from their little town of Preston. People who knew them and knew their story.

He watched as she turned to Erin, and he could almost

hear her say "I don't understand." It was exactly what he had hoped she'd say.

The event was being called "Date Your Neighbors," and the whole town was encouraged to participate. By going from table to table, they were going to get to know their neighbors and find out things about them that they might not have known before. Jace had claimed that he had to work late, so Erin had convinced Isabella to come with her.

"I don't want to go without you," Isabella had said to him. "Besides, I already know everyone in town. I do most of their hair!"

Jace had laughed and told her it would be fun and that it would be a good time for her and Erin to go out. Then he had gone on about how his sister needed to go out more with the girls because she spent way too much time home with either just her husband or Beau. Lucky for him, Isabella had a soft spot for helping people so she'd agreed to go.

And now here they were.

"Attention everyone!" their original speed dating hostess called out. Yes, he had asked her to help him with this little endeavor, and she had been more than thrilled to comply. She was wearing her leopard print again, and if anything, her hair was even bigger than it had been that first night. How it was possible, he had no idea.

"Okay, tonight is very special, and this is the first time we're trying this format, so please just play along! We want to encourage everyone in the community to get to know one another, and we thought this would be a great way to

NOELLE ADAMS & SAMANTHA CHASE

do it. Obviously everyone wouldn't fit in here, but we're thrilled with the turnout."

Jace sighed and wished she'd get on with it already. He was beginning to sweat back here.

"We've assigned half the room with tables, and they are the established families in the community. The rest of you have been given a number of which table you'll start at. You have three minutes per table, and when you get together, you will introduce yourselves, tell each other what you do for a living, and share something that you love about our beloved community and what makes it a great place to live. Are we ready?"

Everyone in the room shouted yes as they cheered and clapped.

"Everyone please go to your first table, and we'll begin in one minute!"

Jace watched as people scrambled and saw Isabella frown as she looked at her number.

Number one.

There were fifteen tables, and he could tell by the look on her face that she was already trying to calculate how long she would be here for. One hour. He had one hour until the event ended.

A hand on his shoulder had him spinning around.

"Here's a glass of water," Vinny, the owner of the bar, said to him. "Now go and get this started."

With a sigh, Jace took a drink and then walked out and made sure he blended into the crowd before he met up with Isabella.

Her smile was wide and welcoming when she spotted him. "You're here! Thank God!" She launched herself into his arms and held him tight. When she pulled back, she looked at him. "Does this mean we can go? I mean, we know everyone."

"Nope," he said lightly, tapping her on the nose. "Let's check this out. Who knows, we may learn some interesting facts about our neighbors tonight."

"Jace, even our parents are here. What are we going to learn about them?"

He shrugged and looked around. "C'mon. It looks like it could be fun. And besides, we're surrounded by friends. How bad could it be?"

She sighed but didn't argue any further. Together they went over to the first table and waited for the bell to ring. When it did, they faced their first neighbor.

It was Mrs. Pendergast.

Isabella playfully elbowed him in the ribs as they smiled at her client. "How are you, Mrs. Pendergast?"

"I'm doing well, doing well," the woman replied as she looked at the two of them. "Do you know one of the greatest things about living in Preston?"

Jace and Isabella shook their heads. "It's the way everyone in town looks out for one another. We may not always agree with each other, but we are protective. It's the kind of community where you'll always feel loved."

They couldn't argue with that, Jace thought. So for the remainder of their time with Mrs. Pendergast, they shared stories of times they'd felt that same way.

Then the bell rang.

Jace's boss sat at the next table. Mr. Channing smiled at them both and took a sip of his drink and said, "Steady employment." Then he nodded his head. "I see great things for you with the town, Jace. I daresay that you'll be taking over my position within the next five years. So you see, that makes Preston a great place to live."

Isabella gave Jace an odd look and then smiled at his boss. "Well, that's good to know. I'd like to think that we'll both always have a good job, and hopefully that will be here in Preston."

The next eight tables it was more of the same—older "hosts" talking about the stability of Preston. It seemed as if most of the local businesses were represented—the caterer, the photography studio, the real estate office, the florist, the printer, and the bakery.

"I guess I had forgotten or not even noticed some of these places," Isabella said as they made their way to the net table. "I'm so focused on the salon and the places that we tend to frequent that I didn't pay attention to all these other businesses."

"Me too. Who knew that our little town had such a variety."

Their next table had Jace's parents, and rather than talk about the town itself, they talked about what it was like to raise a family in Preston—the good schools, the taxes, the cost of owning a home of their own. Jace noticed a look of longing on Isabella's face, and he wrapped an arm around her waist and tucked her in close beside him, kissing her head.

"I know I always appreciated everything you two did for our family," Jace said.

The bell rang out, and Isabella's parents were at the next table. Like his, they shared the joys of raising their family here—adding how much they loved their local church and how they had gotten married there and their other daughters had gotten married there as well. "It's a lovely tradition," her mother said.

"Maybe someday I will too," Isabella said wistfully, but Jace could tell she was fighting to not look up at him as she said it.

The next table sat their neighbors, Heather and Chris. They were both beaming as Jace and Isabella sat down. "Needless to say, we both have a fondness for the town," Heather said as she smiled at Chris. "It's where we first met, and it's the place we both came back to and found each other."

Chris nodded. "Someday we hope to have a house of our own, but for now we're kind of fond of our little apartment in Preston Mill. We've made some great friends and found the direction for our lives. And I can honestly say that without the support of the people around us, it wouldn't have happened."

Jace smiled and nodded too. "You guys are certainly blessed. I remember watching your relationship just from a neighborly standpoint, and I'm so happy to see where you're at now."

Heather hugged Chris and put her head on his shoulder. "And it's only going to get better. The wedding is only a month away, and we can't wait!"

"We are so happy for you both," Isabella said.

"Mrs. Harris' bridal shop has been amazing. I'm telling you, she has been the best person to work with."

The bell rang out, and they wished the other couple a good night, and when they turned, they both sort of paused.

Estelle.

Jace couldn't speak for Isabella, but this was certainly the first time he had seen the older woman without her trademark pink curlers.

"Come on, come on, you two," she snapped at the two of them. "We don't have all night. As it is, I'm missing Wheel of Fortune for this."

Beside him, Isabella groaned, but he nudged her forward. "It's nice to see you here, Mrs. Berry," Jace said. "I would think that you knew everyone here."

"Oh, I do," she said. "But every once in a while, I like to get out and see some fresh faces. It's nice to see the younger generation coming out and taking an interest in local events."

"So," Isabella began, "did you used to work here in Preston when you were younger?"

The question seemed to take Estelle by surprise. "My dear, my husband Edgar—God rest his soul—used to be the mayor of Preston! We were like the first family of this town. I never could imagine living any place else. You see, like most of the people in this room, we met right here in town. Went to school together, became friends, and then we fell in love." Her eyes welled a little with tears. "I'm sure as you made your way around this room, you heard similar tales. There's just something about this place that brings people together."

Isabella snuggled closer to Jace. "Yes it does."

"I've seen it happen, and even though it ain't right the way you young people play the field these days, it's nice when you figure it out sooner rather than later that hanky-panky with too many partners isn't a good thing!" She paused and her eyes narrowed at the two of them. "You ain't hanky-pankying around anymore, are you?"

"What?" Isabella said, almost choking on her response. "No! No, ma'am. We're not. We don't... I mean, it's not..." She looked up at Jace for assistance.

"Excuse me a minute," he said mildly. "I need to get another drink."

As he walked away, he could hear Isabella—in hushed tones—asking him to come back and Estelle talking about young men these days not having manners.

He could live with that.

As he walked toward the bar, the bell rang out, and he knew Isabella would be more than a little annoyed that he wasn't there with her to get to the last table. But he would be.

In a minute.

He saw everyone moving around, and at the bar he grabbed what he'd come for and then made his way back

NOELLE ADAMS & SAMANTHA CHASE

to Isabella who was standing next to an empty table. Jace motioned for her to take a seat on one side, and he took the one opposite her.

"I don't get it," she said when they were both seated. "I could have sworn people were at this table all along."

Jace just shrugged and put his glass down on the table before reaching for her hand. "Doesn't matter. I'm just glad that I'm sitting across from the neighbor that I'm actually dating," he said with a sincere smile. He felt some of his anxiety leave him when she smiled back.

"I have to admit, I thought this was a silly idea, but we definitely heard some great stories here tonight."

He nodded. "We did. We learned that Preston is a great place to meet the love of your life."

She blushed adorably and nodded with him. "That we did."

"And how stable the economy is and how it looks like I'm going to have a job that just might take me into retirement."

Isabella squeezed his hand. "That was brand new information but very cool."

"That one kind of shocked me," he admitted.

"But in a good way, right?"

"Absolutely." He paused and rubbed his thumb over her fingers as he continued to hold her hand. "We learned that there are a lot of amazing businesses here in town that neither of us was fully aware of."

She giggled. "I always got my flowers from the grocery store! Now I'll have to check out the florist."

"You should. You definitely should." He looked into her eyes and just felt peace. "We learned that Preston is a great place to buy a home and raise a family."

"We can personally attest to that. After all, we were both born and raised here."

"I think what I—personally—have come away with from all this, is that Preston is almost perfect."

"Almost?" she said with a small laugh. "How could you say that? Everything we heard tonight was positive."

He shook his head. "Well, I think there's one last thing I would need to hear to make it perfect for me."

Isabella looked at him oddly. "Like what?"

And then Jace stood before dropping to one knee—Isabella's hand still in his. Her soft gasp was her only reaction, and around him he could have heard a pin drop.

"Isabella Warren, tonight we heard about how this town was the perfect place to have a future. But for me, it would only be perfect if it was our future that we were talking about. Together, I want us to plan a wedding, buy a home, have a baby, and grow old surrounded by the loving community that we have right here." He paused and had to resist the urge to wipe away the tears that were slowly rolling down her cheek. "Be my wife, Bella. You're already my everything." Then he chuckled. "Well, you're my everything else. But now, I want you to marry me and have the kind of future we learned about here tonight."

Isabella looked around the room, and he knew the instant she realized that everyone was in on this—they had all moved closer and were watching and waiting for her response. When she turned back to Jace, she nodded. "Yes," she said softly. "Yes, I want to be your wife because, more than anything else, I want to be your everything."

Jace stood and reached into his pocket and pulled out a small velvet box and opened it. Inside was a beautiful princess-cut diamond—one that he knew she favored. "It's always been you, Bella. You complete me."

Isabella's hand stroked his cheek as she smiled at him. "We complete each other." He put the ring on her finger and pulled her close. And when his lips touched hers, the entire room burst out in cheers as the final bell of the night rang out.

Which was perfect to Jace.

He was done dating.

ABOUT NOELLE ADAMS

Noelle handwrote her first romance novel in a spiral-bound notebook when she was twelve, and she hasn't stopped writing since. She has lived in eight different states and currently resides in Virginia, where she writes full time, reads any book she can get her hands on, and offers tribute to a very spoiled cocker spaniel.

She loves travel, art, history, and ice cream. After spending far too many years of her life in graduate school, she has decided to reorient her priorities and focus on writing contemporary romances. For more information, please check out her website: noelle-adams.com.

If you want to keep up with her new releases and sales, you can sign up for her monthly newsletter.

If you want book discussion and insider information on her books, you can join her Reader Group on Facebook. Just ask to join and she'll approve you.

If you want a complete list of her books, including series and tropes, you can go to her Printable Book List.

ABOUT SAMANTHA CHASE

New York Times and USA Today Bestseller/contemporary romance writer Samantha Chase released her debut novel, Jordan's Return, in November 2011. Although she waited until she was in her 40's to publish for the first time, writing has been a lifelong passion. Her motivation to take that step was her students: teaching creative writing to elementary age students all the way up through high school and encouraging those students to follow their writing dreams gave Samantha the confidence to take that step as well.

When she's not working on a new story, she spends her time reading contemporary romances, blogging, playing way too many games of Scrabble on Facebook and spending time with her husband of 25 years and their two sons in North Carolina. For more information visit her website at www.chasing-romance.com.

Sign up for her mailing list and get exclusive content and chances to win members-only prizes!

http://bit.ly/1jqdxPR

Made in the USA
Las Vegas, NV
13 December 2023

82681648R00127